IT TOOK ONLY SECONDS FOR EVERYTHING TO CHANGE

They were passing other cars as if they were standing still. Somebody blew an angry horn at them, and Buddy laughed and made an obscene gesture.

Tom was scared and excited. In the back of his head, though, he thought how mad his mom would be if she could see them tearing along in her new Audi. But he pushed the thought out of his mind.

About half a mile down the road, the accident happened. Buddy was weaving across the center line, and suddenly there were headlights in their faces, brakes screeched, and then came the almost slow crash of metal on metal....

Avon Camelot Books by
Barbara Corcoran

YOU PUT UP WITH ME,
I'LL PUT UP WITH YOU

The Hideaway

BARBARA CORCORAN

AN AVON FLARE BOOK

AVON BOOKS
A division of
The Hearst Corporation
105 Madison Avenue
New York, New York 10016

"A Jean Karl Book"
Copyright © 1987 by Barbara Corcoran
Map by Felicia Bond
Published by arrangement with Atheneum/Macmillan Publishing Company
Library of Congress Catalog Card Number: 86-28849
ISBN: 0-380-70635-0
RL: 4.7

First Avon Flare Printing: June 1989

Printed in the U.S.A.

K-R 10 9 8 7 6 5 4 3 2 1

For Jim

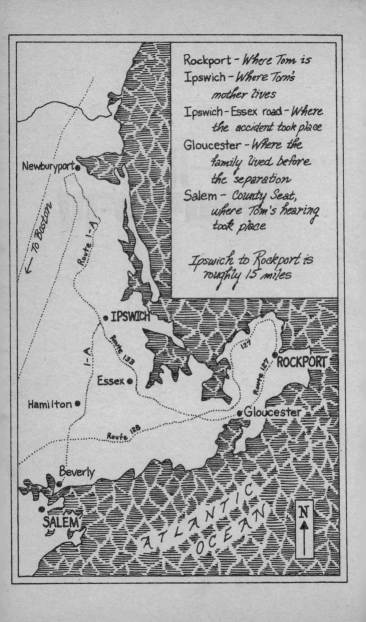

Rockport – *Where Tom is*
Ipswich – *Where Tom's mother lives*
Ipswich-Essex road – *Where the accident took place*
Gloucester – *Where the family lived before the separation*
Salem – *County Seat, where Tom's hearing took place*

Ipswich to Rockport is roughly 15 miles

The Hideaway

1

Tom's stomach muscles clenched as the announcer on the truck's radio said, "And now the state news. . . ." He relaxed again, letting out his breath slowly, as the big guy driving the truck reached over and switched to a rock station.

"News," the driver said, "who needs it!" He gave Tom a wide grin. "Ain't ever good!"

"That's right," Tom said. He hoped his voice didn't sound shaky. He tried to think of something else to say, but the driver was not a chatty man. He was more the kind of guy who whistled between his teeth, and muttered at the idiocy of other drivers.

Maybe a kid running away from the school wasn't big news anyway, but Tony had warned him that the cops around the state would be alerted. "You got to watch out for local fuzz," Tony had said. "Don't get into any trouble, like don't jaywalk or try to buy a beer."

The truck pulled into a truck stop on the edge of town. "Here we go," the driver said.

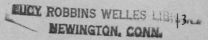
3

Tom grabbed the paper bag he was carrying and reached for the cab handle. "Thanks a lot." He hoped he sounded cool, as if he hitched rides all the time.

"No sweat," the driver said. "You take care now." He swung himself out of the cab and disappeared.

Tom jumped down, feeling panicky. What if the guy went inside and said, "Just gave a ride to some kid, looked as if he was on the lam." And somebody would say, "That must be the kid that ran away from that reform school place." And they would call the cops.

He tucked the bag under his arm and made himself walk normally down the street. He had come away with nothing but his Walkman, which he had sold to buy a wool shirt, a flashlight, and a Swiss knife at The Army and Navy Store in Boston. His windbreaker had gone into a Dumpster; so if they were looking for a fifteen-year-old male, with brown hair, and brown eyes, wearing jeans and a blue windbreaker, maybe the shirt would throw them off.

It was risky coming back to this town, near where the accident had happened, but he had to talk to Buddy. That was the whole point of his escape. He had to get this mess straightened out while the investigation was still going on, before they decided to try him, or just keep him locked up.

He wasn't well-known in this town. He'd stayed last summer with his dad and the Other Woman, while he worked at the theater and then for a little while last spring, while his mom made up her mind whether she was or wasn't going to move in with Archie over in Ipswich. He was pretty sure Archie was the reason his mom refused to let him come home after the accident. Usually kids in trouble got to stay with a parent while the investigation was going on, but his mother threw such a major fit, they'd sent him to the school. His dad probably would have taken him, but the Other Woman put her foot down. "One kid," she said, "is enough." At least that was the conversation as Shelley had written it to him.

He was in the main part of town now, walking briskly without making eye contact, the way Tony had said. "Walk like you know where you're going. If you look like you're unsure of yourself, they nab you." Tony had spent years on the street, and he knew.

He hoped and prayed that Shelley had understood his letter. He'd used the old code they'd made up when they were kids. He'd need Shel's help.

He passed the seafood restaurant, where his dad had taken him for lunch. He smelled the fried clams and home-baked bread; real food, non-institutional food, prepared by experts to please real people. His stomach tightened. He had had only a couple of onion rolls and a cup of coffee since he left. Keeping on the move had seemed safest. Even stopping at The Army and Navy Store in Boston had scared him. He had ended up taking the first shirt on the rack that was his size.

The end-of-summer tourists were almost gone now. The town was beginning to take on its winter look. An elderly couple in a car with Florida plates were parked at the curb, arguing over a map; taking up too much room on the narrow street. A pickup behind them honked irritably and then cut around. The old woman looked up and caught Tom's eye. He knew she was going to ask him for directions. Apologizing to her in his head for being rude, he looked away and quickened his step. He couldn't get into conversations, not even with a lost old lady from Florida. I'm a stranger here myself, lady.

As he came down the street, he smelled the ocean and it made his heart beat fast. He had missed that salty, fishy, head-clearing smell. In Gloucester, where he had lived until his parents broke up, the sea was always right there.

A man leafing through some magazines outside a store that sold newspapers, magazines, candy, cookies, chips, and post-cards, looked up and nodded. "Nice day," he said.

"Real nice." Tom kept going. His voice had changed some more in the four months he'd been away. He wondered if Shelley would notice. She usually noticed things. She'd written him every day for the whole four months. That was pretty good for a thirteen-year-old. Shel had always been his best friend.

He crossed the street and went down the narrow cobblestone road past a lot of little shops, closed now for the season. In summer this place was wall-to-wall tourists, but no one was in sight today. This rocky point of land stuck out into the harbor like a crooked finger. The shacks that housed shops had once been fishermen's homes, his dad said, back when fish instead of people were the main crop. They were still weathered gray shingle buildings, but they had been dressed up by the new tenants—blue shutters, red doors, flowers—all dead with the season over. Bookshops, artists' studios, pottery shops, toy shops, gift shops. Now the silence was broken only by the gulls and the sea.

He looked at the harbor. It was so blue, it made him blink. Boats anchored off the shore rocked gently as if to some faraway music. Jepson, the counselor he had liked at the school, had said that what we remember is always better than what the reality is, but this time Jepson was wrong. The harbor, the water, the boats, the gulls circling, the gray granite rocks that edged the harbor, the salty air, these were all better than he remembered.

He stood leaning against the wall of a gift shop, looking at the harbor and the pier, where a closed-up restaurant advertised FRIED CLAMS, LOBSTER ROLLS, GOOD COFFEE. He picked his way along the narrow edge of the pier between the wall of the restaurant and the water. On the harbor's edge, metal tables with holes for umbrellas were pushed back against the building. He sat down on a piling. A man going by in a sailboat waved, and he waved back. He wondered if his dad still had the catboat. For a moment he thought about sailing out of the harbor into the open sea, the sheets whipping and singing, and wind beating him in the face.

But he couldn't think about things like that now. He was here to talk to Buddy; to get himself out of the stupid mess he was in. He was certain that Buddy didn't realize what had happened to him. Shelley said they didn't use any names in the paper on account of Tom's being a juvenile; and the paper hadn't said he was sent to the school. Buddy spent his summers in Maine, and now he probably was busy getting ready for college. It was understandable that he'd forgotten all about that crazy accident. He probably figured Tom had run away, the same way he had, and that nothing had come of it. Tom had written to him once, not saying much because sometimes the school censored letters. Buddy hadn't written back, but probably the letter had been lost in the mail, or something. He'd known Buddy since they went to the same camp down in Maine. He'd always looked up to him.

It was hard to move. It was peaceful sitting here at the water's edge with no place he had to go, nobody telling him what to do, and no schedule that had to be kept. But the September sun was moving into the west, and the long shadows of afternoon fell aslant the harbor. He had to get settled in. He sighed, got up and made his way to the building at the end of the point.

It was a low stone and cement building without windows, sitting broadside to the harbor. Long ago it had been built by a fish company for packing salt cod, but after it had lain idle for a few years, somebody had leased it for a summer theater. He felt a surge of anger looking at the tattered posters in front. He could probably have gotten a job here again, the way he did last year, painting flats, and running errands, being a general "dogsbody," as the director called him. He had fallen in love with the theater that summer. But this year, instead of a theater job, he had spent the summer at that damned school. Four stupid wasted months, answering psychologists' questions (or evading them some of the time), keeping his room so neat he was named "Best Boy" in the dorm, doing what he was told, and never squealing on Buddy.

He looked back to make sure he wasn't seen. Springing the lock on the door was a piece of cake. He had learned lots of things at the school that were not in the usual high school curriculum. He used the Swiss knife he'd bought at The Army and Navy Store.

Stepping inside, he closed the door behind him. The darkness came down on him, and for a moment he felt panicky. He had always hated darkness. There had been awful fights, when they all lived together, before his father would let him have a night light.

He reached inside the paper bag and took out the flashlight. The strong beam of light made him feel better. It was the same familiar little theater, with about three hundred uncomfortable wooden seats, and at the other end the stage. The ratty old curtain that used to stick had not been replaced, and it was half open. Some furniture, probably used for the production of *Hedda Gabler* that was advertised on the poster, stood on the stage, but the flats were stacked at the back. The stage looked like a forlorn Victorian parlor, whose walls had somehow been blasted away.

But that sofa would do fine for sleeping; and there were a couple of chairs and tables, and an oil lamp. He hoped it had some oil in it, but probably not. He walked slowly down the aisle, and vaulted onto the stage. Playing his light back over the seats, he imagined them filled with applauding people.

He bowed. "Thank you very much." His voice sounded hollow in the empty building. "I'm glad you liked my play. It's written from the heart." Only he wouldn't have Victorian furniture in his play. He'd need beds and desks built of cement, built right into the walls. He'd need bars on windows, and a lot of background noise . . . radios playing, voices arguing, shouting, laughing, crying. . . .

He shook himself, put his paper bag on the dusty table, then set the flashlight on end, where it threw enormous shadows around the stage as he moved. Offstage on either side were the tiny dressing rooms —one for men, one for women—and a bathroom of sorts. The actors had always complained about the backstage conditions, but now they would be his suite, his condo.

He sat on the sofa, sneezing at the cloud of dust that arose, and flipped the tab off the can of Coke in his bag. He had wanted to buy a six-pack, but he hadn't wanted to carry it. Anyway he didn't have much money left. That pawnshop guy had not come through with much. Maybe Shelley could bring him some stuff; if she came. He held his watch to the light, the digital watch his father had sent him last July on his birthday. So he could look at it at school, and tell at a glance what time it was in London and Hong Kong? Dear old Dad, always the brilliant thought. Well, Shelley would say, he means well.

He hadn't seen his parents since the preliminary hearing over at the Salem Court House, in the juvenile court. He remembered looking at his mother's face when the clerk had read out, "In the matter of Thomas James Eaton, a child. . . ." He had never forgotten how anguished she looked. The dispositional hearing, which would determine his punishment, was still pending. "The wheels of justice," his friend Tony had said, "they're square wheels."

He wondered if the parents had been told yet that he had run away. His mom would have one of her hysterical fits, and his dad would sound helpless. He'd say, "It was you he was living with when it happened, Mavis." He wondered how they would react when they found out he had not been driving. Maybe his mother would feel bad, and maybe she wouldn't. She might say, "You let him get you drunk. You gave him the keys to my new car." And she'd call him a fool for taking the rap for Buddy.

But what he figured was, he and Buddy could get together and come up with a story, like how, yeah, Buddy was driving, and yeah, they'd had some vodka, but a tire blew or something, and the accident was unavoidable. Anything, so Buddy wouldn't have to go to jail. He was eighteen, and they'd really nail him; just when he was going to Yale on a baseball scholarship. You couldn't let a guy like Buddy have his life ruined. He just wished, though, that he could have talked to Buddy sooner. Buddy's family went to Maine for the summer, and probably his letter hadn't been forwarded. It didn't say much anyway; but he'd wanted to let Buddy know where he was. This week when he'd been moved to minimum security, he'd decided to go for it. Now he had to find Buddy.

He finished his Coke and threw the can hard across the stage. He wished he could keep from thinking about the guy they had hit. Shel said he was still in a wheelchair. One thing Tom knew for sure, he was never going to drink again as long as he lived. It wasn't worth it.

He thought of Mr. Harris, the director at the school, who had trusted him. He didn't like having to let him down. But he had to run away; it was the only way he could get this mess straightened out.

He stretched out on the sofa to see if it would work as a bed. It wasn't really long enough, but if he crooked his knees, it would do.

He was very tired, and he almost felt like crying. Right now he'd give anything to be home in his mother's house in his own bed, with nobody mad at him.

He fell asleep at last. A moth circled the beam of the upturned flashlight and finally fell onto it. Somewhere in the wings a mouse rattled the flimsy wall of the men's dressing room. The incoming tide slapped the tiny strip of beach below the theater.

2

Shelley put the letter quickly into her pocket.

"Letter from your brother?" the Other Woman said, looking through her own mail.

"No, it's from my cousin George," Shelley said. The Other Woman wouldn't know that George wouldn't be caught dead writing to her. Anyway she knew Enid wouldn't push it; she wasn't really interested in her stepchildren. "There was a phone call for Dad." She gave Enid the number. It had sounded official, and it scared her. She was afraid Tom was in some kind of new trouble. But she didn't tell Enid that the man had said it was urgent.

She went up to her room, locked the door, and opened Tom's letter. It began: "Dear Halfie." That was what he used to call her sometimes, to tease her about not being her real brother, only half a brother. It had bothered her that they weren't complete brother and sister.

The letter went on: "Have some news. I think. If all

goes okay. . . ." And then it went into their old code. She reached for paper and pencil. The code was easy: A Roman numeral and a letter. You moved ahead from the letter to the place in the alphabet that the Roman numeral said. If you said *IV* and then a *b,* the real letter would be *f,* four places ahead of the *b.* Two exclamation points marked the end of a word, one marked off the letter. A question mark was the end of a sentence.

He had written: "I a! IV a!! I z! II r!! I c! II m! III z! III h!! I s! VII a! IV a! I z! I s! IV a! II p!! II r! III r! IV a !!"

She worked it out: "Be at dock theater tue!"

Be at the Dock Theater Tuesday? The Dock Theater here? Tuesday was today. She caught her breath. He was getting out! Wait, hold it. He couldn't be getting out, could he? She thought hard for a minute, pulling her short hair back from her forehead till it hurt. The man who had called for her father had said, "Urgent."

The phone was ringing as she ran down the stairs, grabbed her bike from the porch, and headed toward town. He had to have run away. But he was out! He was *out!*

She looked back to see if anyone was following her. Just to be sure, she circled around a couple of side streets, and stopped at the grocery store for some things. Then she rode her bike over the bumpy cobblestones to the old Dock Theater. The door was closed. There wasn't a sound except for the waves breaking on the little beach at the foot of the point. She looked carefully at the padlock on the door. It had been opened. She took a deep breath and knocked.

3

Someone was knocking on the door. Tom woke up with a lurch of alarm, and for a moment he thought he was back at the school and had slept through the wake-up whistle. When he realized where he was, he thought, *They've found me.* He shook with fear.

Then he heard the three-note whistle, his and Shelley's signal. He bounded off the sofa and ran up the aisle, his heart pounding. His hands shook so much, he had trouble opening the door. At last he got it open, and there she was: Shelley.

For a long moment they stared at each other.

"Halfie," he said softly.

"Hi, Tom." Her voice was small and flat, and she was looking at him with her wide gray-blue eyes as if she didn't believe he was real.

He held out his arms. For a moment she hesitated, then she flew into them. They clung to each other, speechless, for a long minute. His arms ached with the joy of hugging her, his kid sister, the only person in the world who really cared about him. When he let her go, he said, "Come inside so I can shut the door."

They moved down to the stage, where he boosted her up and then turned the flashlight on so they could see each other better. "Well," he said. "What do you know."

"You made it."

"It was easy. I got moved to minimum security. I just walked off campus, and then I got a ride with a truck driver into Boston. It was a cinch. I hitched a ride with another truck that came all the way here."

"You could get murdered hitchhiking." She sat on the edge of the sofa, unable to take her eyes off him.

"Nobody's going to murder me. What for? Anyway I'm pushin' six feet tall, you know."

"They don't go by height."

He laughed. Same old argumentative Shel. Their dad used to say she could argue a person right to the edge of a whirlpool, and then dump him in. "You don't look any different."

"You do. You're older. Your voice is deeper. It's scary."

"Come on, Shel. It's only me." He didn't want her to think he had changed.

"Anyway," she said. "I grew too. An inch."

"I'm impressed." He couldn't seem to relax. "How are you getting along with Dad and the Other Woman?"

"It's okay. They don't pay much attention to me, I don't pay any attention to them. I don't really care whether I'm here or at Mom's." She paused. "Some guy called, he sounded like the cops, or the school, or something."

Tom's stomach tightened. "What'd he say?"

"Just to have Dad call him right away. Urgent, he said."

"Has he called him?"

"Dad's in Boston today. But the phone was ringing when I left. Enid was answering."

Tom thought about it. "He's probably called Mom by now, too."

"You can't stay here very long, Tom."

"Just long enough to talk to Buddy. Then it will be okay."

She frowned. "Buddy!"

"Yeah, Buddy Peterson. I can't tell you about it till I talk to him."

"You haven't told me anything, not about what happened."

"I couldn't. Sometimes they read your mail. Spot-check."

"Tom. . . ."

"Did you come on your bike?" He kept listening for sounds outside.

"Yes."

"I'd better bring it in. I don't want to advertise that I'm here." He wheeled the bike inside and noticed the grocery bag in the carrier. "What you got here?"

"Stuff for you."

"Hey, all right! Boy, do I need it." He carried the bag onstage and began to unload the contents. "Oranges! Plums! Bread, salami, jam, milk. Even a roll of toilet paper. Shel, if I ever go to live on a desert island, remind me to take you along." He was so touched by her thoughtfulness, he wanted to hug her.

"Make a list of whatever else you need." She was studying him. "Tom, why do you want to talk to Buddy?"

"Tell you later."

"I think they're out of town. He may be at college by now."

He felt a lurch of despair. If Buddy wasn't there, what would he do? "Are you sure he's not here?"

"No, but I think so. I can find out."

"As soon as you can, okay?"

"Tom, Buddy got you into that mess, didn't he."

"People get into their own messes." That was what the counselor at school said.

"You always think Buddy's so perfect. Buddy can do no wrong. . . ."

"Never mind, Shel!" He sounded angrier than he meant to, and Shelley's eyes filled with tears.

"He only came around when he wanted to borrow money or something, and you always took him back like he was your long-lost brother."

He felt too depressed to answer. He walked offstage to the grimy little bathroom and leaned against the door, feeling sick. He'd taken the big chance, running away, so he could talk to Buddy and straighten things out. If he couldn't get hold of him, he'd be up a creek. He'd be picked up as a runaway, and he'd never get out of that school.

What Shelley said hurt because he knew it was partly true. Buddy did come around when he wanted something, then ignored him for months. But Buddy was three years older; naturally he hadn't wanted to hang out all the time with a kid younger than he was. Buddy was on the baseball team, and he got good grades. Tom did all right, but he was always glad he wasn't in the same school, where he'd feel competitive. Sure, Buddy was a role model, but what was wrong with that?

And Buddy didn't "get him drunk" that night. Buddy brought the vodka, but Tom didn't have to drink it. He didn't have to get smashed, and he didn't have to go along with Buddy's idea to take Tom's mother's new car for a ride. Buddy had driven because Tom was drunk as a skunk. He remembered thinking, "Wow! Life in the fast lane!" as they tooled along the Ipswich-Essex road, with the sun roof and all the windows open, and the wind in their faces.

It was the fast lane, all right. As soon as they got out of Ipswich, Buddy let 'er rip. He remembered how Buddy's long hair blew back off his face, and how sharp his profile was, like one of those Greek statues at the Fine Arts Museum.

"Let's get us some girls," Buddy had yelled.

They were passing other cars as if they were standing still. Somebody coming out of the live lobster place blew an angry horn at them, and Buddy laughed and made an obscene gesture.

Girls! Buddy must know some really awesome girls, older girls. Tom had been scared and excited. In the back of his head, though, he thought how mad his mom would be if she could see them tearing along in her new Audi; he didn't really want to make her mad, just when they'd kind of gotten sorted out about the guy she wanted to marry. But he had pushed the thought out of his mind.

About half a mile past Lewis's restaurant the accident happened. Buddy was weaving across the center line, and suddenly there were headlights in their faces, brakes screeched, and then came the almost slow crash of metal on metal.

When he came to, he was lying in a ditch. The Audi was totaled, and another car lay on its back, helpless as a turtle that somebody has flipped over. Buddy was nowhere in sight, and there was a siren getting louder. Cars had stopped, and people were running toward the wreck.

Carefully Tom got to his hands and knees and then to his feet. He was cold sober now, and as far as he could tell, no bones were broken. He started running across the marsh, toward the sea. His head ached, there was something wrong with his wrist, and his face stung. All he could think of was that Buddy had been in trouble a couple of times before for driving under the influence, and driving after his license had been taken away. He mustn't let them know Buddy had been driving, or his best friend would be in bad trouble.

It was hard running in the tall marsh grass, and they caught up with him in no time at all. He tried not to worry; it wasn't as if he had a record or anything. He'd never been in trouble. A kid taking his mom's car for a little drive—that might be something your parents would get mad about, but not the law. When they questioned him, he said he had been alone. They gave him an alcohol test. They told him the driver of the car that had been hit thought there were two people in the Audi. He denied it. And then they told him the driver of the other car was hurt bad.

He hadn't even thought about the guy in the other car. All he'd thought about was protecting Buddy and getting away himself till he had time to think. Maybe he could claim amnesia. But when he tried it with the cops, when they were charging him with drunk driving, driving without a license, and leaving the scene, the officer's answer had been short and profane. So after that Tom clammed up. If he didn't answer questions, he wouldn't say the wrong things. Cops never believed kids anyway.

All through the investigation when he was questioned first by the Ipswich police and then by the juvenile court people in Salem, he kept expecting Buddy to come forward and say he had been driving. But he never did, and so Tom was sure Buddy just didn't realize what was happening. Probably he had already gone to Maine for the summer.

When Tom's mother refused to let him stay with her, and they took him across state to the school, he thought he'd hear from Buddy for sure. Finally he wrote that letter. And now Shel was saying Buddy and his folks were still out of town. That probably explained everything. But he had to get hold of him before he left for college. Buddy would have a good idea about how to get both of them off the hook. Buddy was smart. But he had to find him. He *had* to!

4

Shelley was worried. Since she'd told him that Buddy was out of town, Tom seemed to have gone far-off somewhere where she couldn't reach him. He looked white as a sheet. She peeled an orange for him.

"You weren't alone in Mom's car, were you." She tried to sound casual, as if it were not a terribly important question.

He looked at her as if he hadn't heard what she said, so she said it again.

"I never thought you were alone. I couldn't figure you getting smashed and taking off wild like that all by yourself."

He shrugged. "Everybody cuts loose some time."

"Not alone, not you. If I were going to be wild, I'd do it by myself, but you wouldn't."

He put a quarter of the orange into his mouth. He was sitting slumped on the sofa now, his long legs stretched out in front of him.

"Was Buddy with you?"

He chewed the orange slowly and swallowed. "Yeah," he said finally.

"Was he driving?" It was beginning to make more sense.

"Yeah."

"Why didn't you say so?" But she knew without asking. Tom was always that way with people he liked. Once he'd taken a licking from their dad for something she had done, and when she'd tried to tell their dad, he'd said she was just trying to take the rap for Tom. It was Tom who took the rap when people he cared about were in trouble.

"He'd have been in bad trouble. He had a record."

She wanted to shake him. "And what kind of trouble do you think you're in?"

He gave her such a despairing look, she wished she hadn't said it.

She tried to think logically. "Did anybody see you guys? Were there any witnesses or anything?"

"Nah. Except the guy we almost hit when he was coming out of the live lobster place. He shook his fist at us. Blew his horn."

"Maybe I could start a secret investigation. Put an ad in the paper: Reward offered for man whose car was nearly hit by an Audi 5000 on the night the 16th of June coming out of . . . what's the name of that lobster place?"

"Oh, Shel, I don't know." He sounded very tired. "It was months ago. Anyway he couldn't say I wasn't driving."

"I've got to think." She looked around the stage.

"Meantime you need stuff. That flashlight's going to burn out. I can get some candles. Enid's got a whole cupboard full."

"Shel, it's risky."

"Don't worry, I'm very careful." To cheer him up, she said, "Remember when we were little, and we used to shadow suspicious characters, when we lived in Gloucester?"

He gave her a small, reluctant smile. "I remember."

"You got caught, but I never did."

He shivered. "Don't talk about getting caught."

"Tom, maybe you should give yourself up. Tell them the whole story, the truth, and how you were trying to protect Buddy because he was your friend, and. . . ."

He interrupted her impatiently. "They'd never believe it."

"But you've got a clean record. . . ."

"Not any more. Anyway they aren't all that fired up about the truth. They've got a kid, me, that's supposed to be there, and he isn't there, and that makes them look bad. People don't like to look bad." He pulled his shirt collar up around his neck as if he were cold. "They'd throw me into max security. I heard about max from my friend Tony. It's the pits. I'd never get out."

She sighed and stood up. If Tom was feeling depressed, there was no use trying to cheer him up. It never worked. "I'll be back after dark."

"You'd better not be wandering around town after dark, Shel."

"I won't be *wandering*."

"They'll notice you're gone."

"I'll say I have to go to the library for an English assignment. They aren't all that interested anyway. They'll be playing bridge or maybe going out. Enid is very social."

She checked carefully before she wheeled her bike outside. Then she left quickly, purposefully, not looking back. Tom had to be saved, and she was the only one who could do it. She was worried, but at the same time she felt a little like Joan of Arc.

5

He felt lonesome after Shelley had left. He found a broom and swept the stage, remembering how that had been one of his jobs last year. It was funny to think about that time, like remembering a time before he was born. What a lot of dreams he had then. Well, as his dad used to say, the one thing you could count on in life was surprises. And, he would add, mostly unpleasant ones.

The place needed to be aired out. After dark he would open the backstage door. Nobody would see it, unless somebody was down there on that little strand of beach, or in a boat right offshore; and he could check first. He wondered how close a watch the harbormaster kept on the shore. Maybe none at all.

He thought about Shel thinking of candles and stuff. She was efficient. That was something he had never noticed about her, but now that he thought of it, he realized she had always been the competent one. He thought of the time he got stuck up in the apple tree and she got him down.

He thought about dinner at his father's house—Roast beef, maybe, baked potatoes with sour cream and chives, and a salad that was more than a limp piece of lettuce and a wilted carrot—Or maybe baked haddock in that good wine sauce the Other Woman made —or marinated herring, stuffed olives. . . . Maybe Shel could get him some olives and a thick Hershey bar with almonds. She had sent him a box of those when he was in the school.

He told himself how good it felt to be alone. That was one of the bad things about the school, never feeling really alone. In the last week at school he had had a room to himself in the minimum security building, but the hall monitor could come in any time he wanted to, and anyway with all the noise and confusion around him, it was hard to feel alone.

He thought about the guys lining up for chow. That awful food! He wished he could send them a truckload of steaks and oranges and good stuff. Tony had probably never had a real steak in his life. There were a lot of good kids in there, doing time, kids whose parents had kicked them out or given them such a hard time they'd run away and gotten into trouble—kids like Howie Sullivan, who got put away because a gang in his neighborhood beat up on him till he joined them, and then framed him in a 7-11 burglary. Of course he got caught, and the others got away. Howie was a good kid. Maybe later he could send him some bubble gum; Howie was crazy for grape bubble gum, and the school store didn't sell it.

He ate some of the food Shelley had brought him. Three salami sandwiches, an orange, and the quart of milk. All right! He felt better.

He opened the seaside door a crack. The sunset was turning the harbor pink, lavender, and blue-gray. He looked at it for a long time. From the window of his room at the school, all he could see was the K-Mart in the distance.

Cautiously he let himself out the door, and flattened himself against the wall. As far as he could tell, there was no one anywhere in sight. The nearest boats, riding gently at anchor, looked deserted. Ducking low he climbed down the steep slope to the tiny beach. Low tide had left a wet hard-packed surface he could walk on. He climbed onto a rock and lay on his stomach, staring at the water, breathing in the salty air. He felt like a tiny dot in the universe, one subatomic particle; but a particle who could breathe, move, pick up a shell, and scoop up a handful of wet sand. He could take off his shoes and wade in cold water; if he wanted to, he could yell. But not yet. First he had to prove he had a right to be free. And if Buddy was away, that was a problem. But he was never going back to that school, no matter what he had to do to keep out.

He watched a wave break, foam, and curve toward the shore. He could almost feel the sting of the water on his face. He was back in the real world, and he was going to stay there.

6

"**I** think he's lost his mind."

Shelley studied her father's face anxiously. He had been on the phone a long time.

"Run away! I can't believe it." He sat down hard on the dining room chair. Enid brought him a fresh martini.

"Calm down, Jack."

"Calm down! He's my stepson."

"Well, you're not supposed to be responsible for him for the rest of his life. He was living with Mavis when the accident happened. Let her worry about him."

"I've had her on the phone already for forty-five minutes. She's hysterical, as usual."

Enid looked sharply at Shelley. "Didn't you have a letter from Tom today?"

Shelley crossed her fingers under the table. "That was from George."

"Shelley," her father said, "do you know anything about this?"

"Dad, how would I know? He didn't write me all that often, and anyway he wouldn't have told me."

"You two were close."

"But the school censors the mail sometimes. He wouldn't be stupid enough to write 'Hey, guess what, I'm going to run away.'"

Her father grunted and drained the martini.

"Forget it and enjoy your dinner," Enid said. "We have a date to play bridge with the Olsons."

Shelley knew her father was really worried. He loved his kids, just wasn't very effective as a dad. Especially now that he had Enid telling him what to do, think, and feel. He wasn't a very strong man, and he usually underreacted to things, while her mother overreacted. They couldn't help it; it was just the way they were.

She was relieved when the meal was over. She scooped up the kitten her father had given her for her birthday, and took him up to her room. His name was Panic, because he seemed so alarmed by everything, especially at first. She cuddled him against her chest. "I'll take you to meet Tom, maybe tomorrow. Right after school, okay?"

The kitten kneaded his claws against her shirt and purred.

"I'd take you tonight, but I've got too much other stuff to carry." She waited, listening for sounds of the car driving away. It seemed to take them a long time to get started. Enid was a great one for putting on a whole new makeup before she went out.

Finally she heard the garage door open and the Olds start. She waited a few minutes longer, to be sure.

Then she put Panic down and began gathering up the things she was going to take to Tom: A sleeping bag, and the candles (the tall perfumed ones that would burn a long time). She went into the kitchen and looked through the cupboards. Luckily Enid was a food stasher. She'd never miss a couple of cans of tuna fish, a can of pineapple, two cans of french fried onions, some cans of grapefruit juice, and two bottles of cranberry juice.

She loaded everything into two old book bags, and put them in the carrier of the bike. The sleeping bag was rolled up, and she put that on top, tying the cord so it wouldn't bounce off.

When she had everything ready, she put the protesting kitten back in the kitchen and closed the door. She wheeled the bike out, closed the garage door, and took off. It was getting dark, and she had no light on her bike, so she avoided the main street, cutting around on side streets as much as possible.

Tom was changed, she thought. He seemed to have grown from a boy to a man in the months since she had seen him. Something about his manner was different. There was a little frown between his eyes that hadn't been there before, and a wary look in his eyes. She felt as if he had moved away from her somehow, into a world she didn't understand.

If only she could discuss Tom with her new friend Genevieve; but of course that was impossible. She would go to see her though, maybe talk a little about how it felt to grow up. Genevieve was twenty-four. Maybe she could tell what it was like. She wondered if it would be in the paper about Tom running away.

How far did they go about not putting juveniles' names in the paper? Most people had probably forgotten about the accident anyway, except Genevieve and her father.

She should have thought of towels. He couldn't take a shower, but still he would need a towel. She'd bring some tomorrow after school. She wondered how long he thought he could stay in that theater building.

On an impulse she stopped and got him a pizza; first parking the bike out of sight behind the pizza parlor.

She was glad she had thought of it when she saw how his face lit up.

"I haven't had a pizza for months," he said, opening it up and inhaling the smell. "Wow, black olives and pepperoni, my favorite. Want a piece?"

She shook her head. "I wish I could bring you a hot shower."

"Do I look filthy?"

"No, I was just thinking how you used to stay in the shower every morning for about half an hour."

He grinned. "With you pounding on the door. Lucky for me nobody turned off the water here. And lucky for them I'm here. In a couple months those pipes could freeze."

"Couple of months! Tom, you aren't planning on staying that long."

"I'm not planning, period. Somehow I have to get hold of Buddy. Can you find out where they are?"

"I'll try. Maybe Ginna Fifield would know. I think she used to date him."

"If I can get a letter to him. . . ."

Shelley didn't feel all that confident about Buddy's

help, but she didn't want to discourage him. "I'll bring my kitten to meet you tomorrow."

"Yeah, you wrote me about the kitten. What's his name?"

"Panic." She went to the stage door and opened it.

"Hey, take it easy. Somebody might see the candle-light."

She closed the door. "There's nobody out there except an old man messing around with his outboard motor, and he didn't even look up."

"What kind of an old man?"

"Just an old man. It's so dark, I can hardly see him anyway. Don't get paranoid."

"You'd get paranoid if you. . . ." His voice was sharp, but he stopped. "Sorry. I'm just jumpy."

"That's okay." She picked up the empty pizza box and threw it in a battered old trash can in one of the dressing rooms. "I've got to go. I'll come tomorrow after school."

When she went out the front door, she fixed the padlock so that to a casual observer it would look as if it were locked. She picked up her bike and started up the street.

A car turned into the cobbled street, which was just wide enough for one way traffic. She tried to duck away from the headlights, but the best she could do was to pull up against the front of a gift shop. The lights caught her for a moment, and the car stopped. She didn't move. It was a police car.

The policeman got out and came over to her. "Evening," he said.

"Hello." She spoke more loudly than normal, praying that Tom would hear their voices and put out the candles.

"What are you doing down here after dark?"

"I . . . I saw a cat run down the street and I thought maybe it was lost. I have a cat myself, and I like cats. . . ." She was sounding like a dumb little kid, but that was all right.

"You'll never find a cat down here, unless it wants you to, and usually they don't. Got a light on that bike?"

"No. I'm just going to wheel it home."

He shoved his hat onto the back of his head. He was young and big. "Where's home?"

She thought of giving him a fake address, but that might cause worse trouble. She gave him the street and number.

"What's your name?" At least he wasn't writing it down. He played his flashlight around the area, and then he walked over to the theater door. "That lock's been picked." He turned to look at her. "You shouldn't be down here, sister. You could get into bad trouble."

Shelley held her breath as he pushed open the door. She couldn't see any light inside. The policeman stepped in and beamed his light around the auditorium.

"Good place for bums to hang out," he said over his shoulder. "Not a good place for you, sister." He pulled the door shut. "We'll put your bike in the trunk, and I'll just give you a ride home."

"You don't need to. . . ."

But he was already boosting the bike into the trunk, tying the trunk lid half shut. He opened the passenger door, and she got in. She was shaking with relief. Tom must have heard him; he must have hidden.

It would have been exciting to ride through town in a police car if she hadn't been worried. The cop would tell whoever owned the building to put a new lock on it. They might find Tom. She hoped Tom had heard what he said, so he'd be careful.

The police car pulled up in front of her house, and she wished her friend Margie could see her. Only of course she didn't really, because Margie would want to know what was going on, and that would mean another lie.

The cop took the bike out and wheeled it to her. "There you go. Are your folks home?"

"They will be in a few minutes."

"You tell 'em the p'lice said not to let you go out after dark by yourself, understand?"

"Okay, thanks very much. I will."

He waited while she wheeled the bike into the garage and went into the house. Then the car slid smoothly away.

She sank into a kitchen chair, and the kitten leaped into her lap. "Wow!" she said. "That was too close."

Panic tucked his head under her arm and purred.

7

Long after he heard the police car drive away, Tom stayed huddled under a row of seats at the far side of the auditorium. That had been too close. If the cop had been a little more thorough with that flashlight, he'd have seen all the stuff on the stage —the food, the Coke can, the candles, the sleeping bag. Maybe he'd come back. Tom decided not to light the candles again tonight.

Shelley was right, he couldn't stay here forever. He would have to figure out something. Maybe he could get up to Canada somehow. He had that fake driver's license that Joe Magone had made for him in the shop just for the fun of it. It was pretty convincing. Joe had cut the head and shoulders out of a snapshot Tom had of Shelley and himself. He laminated it, and printed in a phony name, Harold Batchelder. The birthdate made him seventeen. The license number was a mix of Joe's number and some figures Tom had come up with, and the address was a phony, 24 Comstock Circle, Topsfield, Massachusetts. Joe said if he was outside, he would have cooked up a real name and address from some guy that was dead; that was how he usually did it. Joe was smart at that kind of stuff; not smart enough, though, to keep out of the school. Tom knew he would never have the nerve for that kind of stuff. And he wouldn't like living on the edge of panic all the time. Panic—that was a funny name for Shelley to give her kitten.

He rolled out from his hiding place and brushed the dust off his clothes. He felt restless and nervous. What if that cop came back for another look? What if he asked Shelley a lot of questions and got suspicious?

Pacing up and down the stage in the dark, he bumped into the sofa and bruised his ankle. He felt like a caged animal. It seemed to him he could smell his own fear.

What if whoever owned this building came over to put a new lock on the door, and found the place occupied? He'd have to run. So he'd better think about where he'd run to. If only he had a boat, it would be easier. Maybe he ought to clear out right now, while it was dark. But he had only about seven dollars. If he waited, maybe Shel could give him a few more bucks. He felt paralyzed by indecision. If Tony were here, or Joe, or some of the other guys at the school, they could give him advice. For a moment he longed for the safety of his tiny room at the school, barred windows and all. But only for a moment.

Cautiously he opened the back door and looked out at the night. There were no stars. The silvery surface of the sea where it broke into waves was barely visible.

He wished he could go for a swim in all that blackness, but somebody might come and he wouldn't even hear them. It was hard to make decisions when you hadn't been able to make them for four months. In one way he hadn't made them for his whole life, not big life and death decisions. Parents made them for you.

He took a deep breath of night air and closed the door. Better bring his sleeping bag and put it close to the door so that if he heard anyone, he could get out fast. No point in undressing.

He was afraid to go to sleep. He lay on the floor listening for sounds. When his watch showed one thirty, he decided it was safe to go to sleep, but still it was hard to unwind. The back of his neck ached with tension, and the outgrown jeans were too tight. He turned and turned, trying to get comfortable.

Just as he was falling asleep, he thought, *What if Buddy won't help me? What if he meant to leave me holding the bag?* But that was too awful to consider. He turned on his stomach and slept uneasily, waking up with a start every half hour or so.

When he woke for good, it was a little after six. He felt cramped, so he got up and opened the back door. The dawn was just starting to lighten the sky. The tide was in; he could hear the slap and rustle of the water on the rocks. He ran in place for a few minutes, his muscles aching and sore.

On an impulse he stripped to his shorts and half climbed, half slid down the embankment to the water where he plunged in, gasping at the cold, and swam into deep water. In spite of the chill, it felt wonderful to be exercising. He swam out to one of the boats, an old outboard, and clung to it for a moment, wishing it were his. ALLIE MAE was painted on the side in faded letters.

The eastern sky was streaked with pink as he swam back to shore. He was starving; all he could think of was bacon and eggs, pancakes, buttered toast, and hot coffee. For a crazy minute he thought about going uptown to an all night cafe he remembered. But that would be too risky.

Back in the theater he towelled himself dry with his T-shirt, and finished off the loaf of bread with some of the raspberry jam Shelley had brought, two oranges, and a plum. He wished he could make some coffee. At school he'd gotten the coffee habit. It was one of the few things the cook did a good job with—coffee, pancakes, and corned beef hash—that was about his limit. Tom scooped up the crumbs on the table and threw them offstage. Breakfast for the mice.

He swept the set, more from the habit acquired at the school than from necessity. They were very strict about neatness. The kids got points for everything, and Tom always got maximum points for cleanliness. He liked keeping his room neat and making his bed the army way.

He swept the dust into the broken dustpan he had found backstage. If he could stay here a while, he could set up those flats, make the place look like a real room. There might be some leftover paint back there, and he could really spruce the place up.

Stooping over the dustpan, he suddenly froze. Someone was knocking on the stage door. He was afraid to move. Someone must have seen him swimming. That had been stupid. They might have called the cops.

The knock came again, a light sound. Police didn't sound like that. They knocked hard and loud. This sound seemed almost apologetic.

A voice said, "Hello? Anybody home?"

That was definitely not what cops said. Tom went to the door and opened it a crack. An old man with white hair stood there holding two Styrofoam cups.

"Mornin'," the man said. "Saw you swimming and thought you might enjoy a cup of coffee with me. That water's a mite chilly."

Tom hesitated and then opened the door further. What kind of trap was this? "Sure. Come on in." He couldn't leave the old guy standing there.

The old man was small and thin, and his pale blue eyes looked friendly.

"That's great," Tom said. "Have a seat."

The man looked around. "Real cozy place you got fixed up here."

"Oh, just passing through," Tom said.

The man sat down on the sofa and put the cups on the table. "Have some java. That's what they used to call it in the old days. Java. Don't know why, unless that's where the beans come from."

"Thanks." Tom took the coffee gratefully. It smelled good. He took a sip and then drank half of it. "Wow. I was wishing for a good cup of coffee." he smiled at the old man. "Java."

"Nothin' like it on a cool mornin'." The man leaned back. "I was down in the cove, paintin'."

"Painting?" What was there to paint in the cove? Maybe the old guy was crazy.

"Paintin' Joe Fellows's catboat, anchored out there near the buoy. I said to myself, that's pretty as a picture, so I painted it."

"Oh, that kind of painting."

The man chuckled. "Not much of the other kind in the cove. My name's Harv."

"Mine's Tom," Tom said, and immediately wished he had made up a name like Howie, or George, or something. Who was this old man anyway?

Harv chatted easily about the weather, about his problems with his outboard, and about the fish he had caught. "Could you use some redfish? They're a mite oily, but I like 'em. You got any place to cook?" He glanced around.

"No, I'm . . . uh . . . kind of camping out for a few days."

"Sure thing. Well, if you like fish, I'll fry some up and bring 'em over."

"Well, that's nice of you, but. . . ." Tom was torn. He would love some good fresh fish, but he didn't want this guy hanging around. "I guess you wonder what I'm doing here. . . ."

Harv stopped him. "Son, I quit wondering about other folks' business a long way back. I figured since I didn't want 'em poking' their noses into mine, I'd better keep my nose out of theirs."

Tom began to relax. The man looked as if he meant what he said, and he didn't look like any kind of cop. "Sure, I'd love some fish."

"Right." Harv stood up. He came about to Tom's

shoulder. "I'll bring 'em over this afternoon, maybe about four."

"Great. I'd appreciate that." Tom walked to the door with him. "Thanks a lot for the coffee."

Harv waved his hand. "No thanks needed. I get kind of lonesome, talking to myself. Not used to it, thought I ought to be by now. See you later." And he was gone, scrambling agilely down the slope and striding off toward the cove.

Tom watched him go. He didn't know what to think. The guy seemed harmless, and he hadn't asked any questions. Still, it made him nervous to have anyone know he was here.

He worried about it off and on all day till Shelley showed up with her kitten, three chili dogs, a bag of Doritos, some bananas, and half a gallon of milk. When he saw what she had in her pocket, he had new things to worry about.

8

Shelley spread the morning paper out on the table, folded to a column that was headed *Your Roving Reporter*. The next to last paragraph was marked in ink. Tom read it over twice.

> Your Roving Reporter has learned that the Ipswich juvenile involved in the drunk-driving escapade that put newspaperman Mort Barton in a wheelchair, maybe permanently, has escaped from the school for delinquent boys where he was being held pending investigation by the juvenile court. One more runaway for the police to cope with.

Tom felt like being sick. He put his hand over his mouth and closed his eyes.

"Daddy asked me a thousand questions. The cops came to see him, and that juvenile guy who's been investigating you. He said he'd finally got a hearing scheduled for you for next week, and now you were gone. He was mad."

"What'd you say?"

"Said I hadn't heard from you lately. I'm getting to be a good liar." She hated to lie; it made her feel yucky, and anyway she was always afraid she'd give herself away.

"Did he believe you?"

"I think so."

"What if they're watching you?"

"I thought of that. I came here by a very screwed-up route, and nobody followed me. Eat your chili dogs before they get cold."

Slowly he unwrapped the chili dogs. He told her about the old man named Harv. When he mentioned the painting, she said, "That must be Genevieve's old man."

"Who's Genevieve?"

She hadn't intended to mention Genevieve yet. "Oh, she's just this woman I met. She's real nice. She's an artist and she gives lessons. She told me she has this old guy who just took up painting and is pretty good."

"He's coming back. To bring me some fish. I wonder if he's checking up."

"What's to check up? Did he ask questions?"

"Not really. I said he must be wondering what I was doing here, and he said he didn't like people being nosy about his business, so he wasn't nosy about theirs."

"Then let it go. Believe him."

"I can't believe people any more."

"Tom, you have to. You have to decide who you can

44|

trust and who you can't." His suspiciousness worried her. He'd never been like that. "You can't go through life thinking everybody's out to get you."

"Well, they were out to get me, and they got me."

"That was your own fault. You ran away, and then you let them think you were alone in the car. I mean you really walked into it."

He looked angry. "I don't squeal on my friends."

"Friends, shmends. Buddy left you holding the bag, and you let him." From the look on his face she decided she had better change the subject, although some time they were going to have to talk about this. "How did Harv know there was anybody here?"

"He saw me swimming."

"Swimming!"

Defensively he said, "I have to get some exercise, don't I? I can't stay cooped up here forever. Anyway it was practically before dawn."

She was trying to think. "There's nothing wrong with a kid going swimming, but if they see you coming back in here. . . . That cop said he was going to tell the owners to put a new lock on the door."

"If it's the same owners, it's a corporation in Boston. They aren't going to worry about a padlock."

"It must be awful cold swimming before dawn. You might get a cramp and drown."

"Tough luck." Morosely he bit into the second hot dog. "Maybe I ought to clear out."

"Not, now. Wait till the news dies down."

"I'm a sitting duck here."

"Well, you'd be a walking duck outside. Where would you go?"

He shrugged. "I know guys that live on the streets all the time."

"And where are they now? Caught and in the school. Anyway it's probably something you have to learn how to do."

"I could learn. I'm not stupid."

She could see this was not the time to argue. She found Panic, who was investigating the trash can. "I'll be back tomorrow. Just be patient and lie low. Is there anything special you want?"

"Yeah," he growled. "A room of my own. A hot shower, three hot meals a day, a refrigerator with snacks, a basketball game, and a decent life."

"Oh, Tom." Her eyes filled with tears.

He saw the tears. "Hey, I'm sorry." He got up. "I didn't mean to yell at you. You're my only friend. The hot dogs were great. Listen, don't worry, all right?"

"All right." She wiped the tears away with the back of her hand. "Just promise you won't leave."

"I promise."

She let herself out carefully, again fixing the padlock so it looked locked. She looked around in all directions before she picked up her bike and started home.

The plan that had been evolving in the back of her mind was going to need attention right away. Her father and Enid had gone to Boston with the Gilmores for dinner and a play, so she had the evening to herself. She had to think.

9

Tom woke up scared. The theater was totally dark and something was banging. He was sure he had left one candle burning when he went to sleep. He lay rigid in his sleeping bag, on the sofa, afraid to move.

As he came more fully awake, he realized that the noise was the stage door banging. He could hear the wind whistling around the building. He sat up and put his feet on the cold floor. He must have forgotten to latch that door after Harv went home, and the wind had blown out the candle.

Still, he moved cautiously, alert to any strange sounds, his hands out in front of him. He fumbled around on the table until he found a book of matches, and one of the candles. His hands were shaking so much that twice he had to light another match.

When he finally had the candle lit, he held it high so he could see better. Nothing seemed to be wrong. Just the open door. He caught and closed it, then leaned against the wall in relief. Harv had stayed a while after he brought the fish, talking about his years in the navy and later as a fisherman. He was good company, and Tom had enjoyed him. But he should have remembered to latch that door.

Something clattered outside. He flattened himself against the wall. Nothing happened. It made him mad that he was freaking out this way over every little thing. When the guys at the school talked about times they'd been on the run, they never sounded as if they were scared. He must be some kind of chicken.

He took a deep breath and pulled the door open fast. There was nothing there but the night and the wind. The sky, scoured clean of clouds, blazed with stars, and down below him the waves hit the shore with a low growl. He could see the pale disturbance of air caused by the tossed spray. It was hurricane season, but the wind tonight was more like a gale than a hurricane.

He stood there breathing deeply, trying to wash the panic out of him. Maybe he'd go for a quick swim, and show himself he wasn't all that scared.

He pulled off his T-shirt and went outside. As he closed the door, the candle blew out. But that was okay, he'd light it again when he came back in. He hadn't looked to see what time it was. It must be near morning.

He slid down the bank fast and plunged into the water without pausing. The cold made him gasp. He struck out at once to warm up. Even here in the cove the surf was heavier than usual. He cut through the water with strong strokes, thinking about a TV thing he had seen once about people who called themselves the Polar Bear Club. They swam all winter off Coney Island. They must be crazy. The cold water felt good though; it cleared the sleep out of his head in a hurry.

Harv made the navy sound like a pretty good life. Maybe Tom ought to join up, use a fake name, and lie about his age. Harv said he'd spent two months in the brig once, but he didn't say what for. Tom had ached to tell him about the school, and the trouble he was in, but of course he couldn't. Harv seemed like a real nice guy, but you couldn't tell about anybody.

He coughed as a wave hit him in the face. The water didn't seem so cold now, and it felt good to be using his muscles.

He swam for a long time without thinking at all. When he began to feel tired, he looked back and realized that he had gone further than he had meant to. He made a wide half circle and started back. Going in was not so easy. The rough water tossed him around, and he could feel the current dragging his feet seaward. He put extra strength into his stroke, but it was still slow going.

The cold was beginning to get to him, and he felt a touch of alarm. The sun would be up pretty soon, and maybe he'd feel warmer. He should have watched how far out he was going. He'd forgotten to allow for the numbing effect of the cold water.

He lifted his head to look at the rocky promontory that jutted out into the water. It seemed as far away as it had been when he turned. He was scared. His life was a mess, but he didn't want to throw it away in icy water in the small hours of the morning. He gulped air and cleaved the water with his arms. His arms and legs were getting numb, and he couldn't seem to get them to do what he wanted them to do.

For a moment he floated facedown, in the dead man's float they used to do at camp. For a vivid second he saw the face of his cabin mate at that camp, old Jody, killed in a skiing accident five years ago. Then Jody's face was gone, and he was striking out again toward shore, trying to fight the current that pulled him the other way. It was getting harder, and he was gasping. He thrashed wildly for a minute. Then he gritted his teeth and made himself calm down. A wave hit him in the face, and he swallowed cold salt water.

He wasn't going to make it. The realization hit him with such force that for a moment he stopped trying to swim.

His leg hit against something, and he grabbed for it, not knowing or caring what it was. He shook the water out of his face and discovered he was hanging onto a buoy that marked the channel just outside the cove. He wrapped his arms around it and hung on, almost crying with relief. He was shivering so much, his teeth chattered. But he didn't care; he was safe.

The buoy bobbed with the waves. One minute he would be half out of the water, the next minute a wave would break over his shoulders and sometimes over his head. Time went by. Downshore a fishing boat sputtered and started, and a minute later he saw it heading out to sea. He yelled and waved, but the men in the boat didn't see him.

The sky was getting lighter. His legs were past feeling, but he exercised his arms as much as he could without letting go of the buoy. He couldn't remember ever being so cold in his life.

Just inside the mouth of the cove the ALLIE MAE rode up and down on the tide. Tom tried to figure if he could swim to the boat. Ordinarily it would be a cinch, but his legs were so paralyzed, he wasn't sure he could make it. His shoulders and arms ached with cold. And what would he do if he did make it? He was sure there weren't any oars in the boat, and he couldn't start the motor, he was sure of that. It was bound to be locked up some way, or maybe Harv took the motor ashore when he wasn't using the boat. It was Harv's boat; he had found that out last night. Maybe when it got light, Harv would come out. He said he still went fishing most days. But would he go in a gale like this if he didn't have to? It didn't seem likely.

As time went by, Tom grew discouraged again. He was afraid he was going to pass out, or at least get so cold he wouldn't be able to hang on to the buoy. He yelled, more for the feeling it gave him of still being alive than for any hope he'd be heard. He carefully let go of the buoy with one hand and waved it violently, then changed hands, trying to get the circulation stirred up. It began to be hard to think about anything except how cold he was. And how hopeless his situation seemed. Shelley was the only one who would miss him, and she wouldn't be around till the middle of the afternoon, when school was out. He thought about his mother, and wondered if she would feel bad when she heard he had drowned. She had cried a lot after the accident, and she had written him long letters at the

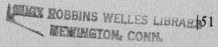

school, mostly saying, "How could you have done this to me?" When he was younger, though, they had been good friends. She used to take him to the theater in Boston sometimes, and she was the one who'd gotten him the job in the summer theater. She'd always wanted to be an actress, but she got married too young, and then Tom's father had died. She had to get a job to support Tom and herself, till she married Shelley's dad, Tom's stepfather, who seemed more real to Tom as a father than his own dad. He hung on to the buoy, wishing he had spent more time with his stepfather.

Twice he slipped into unconsciousness, and each time a wave smacked him back. The second time he almost lost hold of the buoy. It would be easy to let go and just drift.

Somewhere close to him, somebody yelled. Seconds later he was conscious of being dragged over the side of a boat. He fell into the wet, fishy-smelling stern, hitting his head on the stern seat.

The next thing he was aware of was being lifted out of the boat, and he stood up on a sandy bottom. His knees buckled, but someone grabbed him.

A voice that seemed far off said, "You know this kid, Harv?"

And he heard Harv's voice saying, "Sure do. He's stayin' with me for a few days."

"Well, you better tie him down," the first voice said. "You darn near lost him. When he comes to, tell him the Atlantic Ocean ain't any swimming pool."

10

Something was wrong. At first he thought it was the silence. He frowned at the raftered ceiling over his head. The wind had died down; that was one thing. Just as he was thinking that, surf broke somewhere with a dull roar, so close to him that he sat up suddenly. His head spun.

He was on a narrow cot with two blankets over him. A big towel was tied around his waist, and his shorts were hung over the back of a kitchen chair, in front of a small black stove where wood was burning. There was a big Band-Aid on his forehead. He coughed, and his chest hurt.

He remembered then where he had been, hanging onto that slippery buoy. He pulled the blankets up around his neck, shuddering. He remembered being hauled into a boat, voices, and being half carried, half dragged.

But where was he? Wherever it was, he had to get out of here. He struggled to his feet. Around him lay a small, neat one-room place that had a corner with a two-burner hot plate and a toaster oven, and a small partitioned-off area that seemed to be a bathroom with a shower. The only furniture was a small table, the kitchen chair, an old leather armchair, and an easel. Several watercolors of the harbor were tacked up on the wall. On the table there were a pair of snapshots, one of a woman standing with her arms folded squinting and smiling at the camera, and one of two boys, about eight and ten, taken a long time ago judging by their clothes.

A newspaper lay on the table. It was the same edition that had the story about him. This must be Harv's place, and Harv had figured out who he was. *Where was Harv?*

He grabbed his sopping wet shorts off the chair and began to put them on. The door opened, and Harv came in, carrying two big paper bags.

"Don't put on them wet pants," Harv said. "You'll catch your death. I took the liberty of stoppin' by your place and gettin' you some dry duds. Here you go." He tossed one of the bags at Tom, and put the other on the table. "While I was over there, I put one of my padlocks on that front door. Not many folks come down that way in winter, but you never know, so many poor souls wanderin' around the country without a place to sleep these days. And who knows but Johnny Marston might take a notion to check on it, though goodness knows, he's not much for bothering. Does a bit of caretakin' for different folks and don't wear himself out over it." As he talked, Harv was taking things out of the paper bag and setting them on the table. "Got us some grub at Ned's place. Ham and eggs, some of Mabel's cinnamon rolls, coffee. . . ." He put paper plates and small plastic knives and forks and spoons on the table.

Hastily Tom got into the jeans and shirt that Harv had brought. He had even remembered socks and sneakers. "That food smells terrific." He couldn't remember ever being so hungry.

"Well, set yourself down and tuck in." Harv picked up the wet shorts, spread them out on the fender of the stove, and pulled the chair up to the table. He brought a small nail keg from the kitchen area and sat on that himself.

For a few minutes Tom ate without speaking. When he began to feel better, he leaned back in the chair and looked at Harv. "I swam out too far."

"I guess you could say that."

Tom flushed. "It was stupid."

"I guess you know that now, so you don't need somebody to tell you."

"Thanks for saving my life."

"That wasn't me, that was Arnie. Good thing Arnie's foolish too, otherwise he wouldn't have been goin' fishing on a day like this mornin' was. That wind was a zinger. All quiet now though, except for the way that high water's smashin' in."

Tom couldn't think of anything more to say. He felt bad about having suspected Harv. Harv was a really nice guy. He put the last of the little paper cup of marmalade on the last piece of toast. "You got a neat place here."

"Used to be the Nelsons' boat house. I fixed it up

and rent it from 'em and kind of looking after their place when they're in Florida."

"It's great. I'd like a place like this." He nodded toward the watercolors on the wall. "Did you paint those?"

"Yep."

"They're nice. I like them." He wanted to ask about that woman Shelley had mentioned, the artist, but he couldn't think of her name, and anyway it was best not to blab away about things.

Harv poured them both some more coffee. "You could hang out here for a spell if you had a mind to. I get sick of talking to myself."

"That's nice of you."

"You can think about it." He went on talking about the storm, and about fishing prospects.

Tom was thinking. It was tempting. He liked this little place. He could set up his sleeping bag over there by the door. All his instincts told him to trust Harv, but the education he had had in the last few months told him not to trust anybody. To change the subject he nodded toward the snapshots and said, "Are those your boys?"

"Yep."

"Do they live around here?"

"Nope. The oldest one lives in Oregon. I was out to see him last year. Nice place, Oregon." He didn't offer any information about the other boy. "You like to play checkers?"

"Yeah, sure. Haven't played since I was a kid." Maybe he's trying to keep me here till the cops come, Tom thought. Maybe it's a trap. But he sat still while

Harv got out an old checkerboard and set it up on the table.

Harv smoked his pipe while he played a shrewd game of checkers, and talked some more about his life at sea. "Morocco," he said, "now there was a mighty interestin' place."

Tom listened to his stories of veiled women and narrow wicked-looking streets, wondering if it was all true or made-up. Harv got up and brought him a dagger in a tooled-leather scabbard. "Brought that back for my boy when he was about your age. His mother said it was a durned fool thing to give a kid." He chuckled but he looked said.

"Was that the boy in Oregon?"

"No, the other one." About fifteen minutes later Harv said, "Talked a lot about being a free spirit, my boy did. That was back in the Sixties, you know, when being free was all the thing."

"Doesn't everybody want to be free?" Tom said. "I sure do. I mean who wants to be stuck in an office nine to five and work himself into a coronary to pay the mortgage?"

Harv didn't answer for a minute. He checkmated Tom and grinned at him. Then he said, "It don't have to be nine to five. Not if that ain't your idea of fun. But I don't know if there's such a thing as real free."

"You seem pretty free yourself."

Harv looked at him from under his bushy eyebrows. "Boy, I'm seventy-three years old. Not so much free as worn out." He lined up the checkers. "Nothing free about the navy. Nothing at all. Nothing free about fishing for a living either." He moved one of the checkers. "*Free* always costs. Somebody always has to pay."

Tom thought about it. "What do you mean?"

Harv relit his pipe. "My boy that wanted so bad to be free, that thought not working and not getting tied to anybody meant free, he died in an alcoholic ward. And it killed his mother." He moved his checker two jumps. "Got ya."

Tom was upset. He felt threatened by something, and he didn't know what it was. He thought about some of the kids at the school: Johnny Fallaci, whose mother used to beat him senseless; Butch Hill, raped by his stepfather all the time; his friend Tony, homeless and living on the street. And they were all shut up in the school now. What were you supposed to do?

Harv stacked his checkers carefully in front of him. "You take kids, now. A kid gets to thinking he's grown-up, ought to be free to act like a grown-up. So maybe he gets a little drunk and smashes up a car, and somebody gets bad hurt . . . Who's free?"

Tom shoved his chair back and stood up so fast that he knocked the checkerboard onto the floor. Harv stopped to pick it up. "It's a trap," Tom said. "You got me here and you're waiting for the cops. . . . I'm getting out of here." He started for the door.

Harv let him get almost there before he spoke. "It ain't any trap. If I was you, I'd come back and set yourself down."

Tom opened the door and looked out. The sea looked cold and gray under a lowering sky. He hesitated. Where would he go?

"Come on back. You didn't finish the game."

Slowly Tom closed the door. "You swear you aren't setting me up?"

Harv looked at him and shook his head. "Do I look to you like a feller that sets up his friends?"

"I'm not your friend. You hardly know me."

"Come back and sit down and quit arguing. Just like my boys, always got to have the last word." But Harv was smiling at him. "Stubborn as ten mules."

"You didn't swear."

"Ain't a swearin' kind of feller, can't you tell?" He chuckled. "And if you believe that lie, you're crazy. Ever meet a man that spent thirty years in the navy and didn't swear?"

Tom came back and sat down. "I wasn't driving. That's why I ran away and came back. I want to prove I wasn't driving."

"Why don't you tell me about it," Harv said.

Tom took a deep breath and began.

11

Shelley watched Ginna Fifield lob a ball into her opponent's court. Shelley had been hanging around the courts for almost half an hour, hoping she could speak to Ginna. At school she had found out for sure that Ginna used to date Buddy Peterson, and that she heard from him sometimes. She didn't want to look as if she were hanging around, so she rode up the street again and went into the little grocery store and bought a Coke.

Just as she began to drink it, she saw Ginna and her friend start off the court. She threw the nearly full bottle into a trash can, and rode her bike back to the court, just as Ginna reached her car. It was scary to speak to her; she was a senior and very popular. Shelley had never even said *"hi"* to her before.

"Ginna?" Shelley walked her bike to the car. Luckily Ginna's friend had gone off in his own car. "Excuse me. . ."

Ginna leaned out and looked at her. "Hi. Do I know you?"

"Probably not. I just wanted to ask you. . . . Somebody said you knew Buddy Peterson's family's address in Maine. My mom wants to write to his mom, and she's lost the address. . . ."

"Oh. Sure." Ginna reached into her purse and pulled out a small address book. She ripped a blank page out of the back, and copied something down. "There you go. Address and phone number, in case they want to shoot the breeze." She gave Shelley a friendly smile and started her car.

"Thanks! Really, thanks a lot."

Ginna was gone. Shelley looked at the scrawled piece of paper. She really had the phone number! Now Tom could call up Buddy. Maybe Buddy would come through, if he was there. She should have asked if he'd gone to New Haven yet. If he had, Tom could get his number from his mother. She could hardly wait to tell Tom. Then that would be okay, and she'd bring up the subject of Genevieve and her dad, and everything would get straightened out. She rode fast toward the Dock Theater.

It was a new padlock, and it was securely locked. She didn't know what to make of it. She knocked hard and gave their old whistle, but nothing happened.

She went around to the stage door. It was locked too, but there was a printed note: "ALL IS WELL. I'LL BE IN TOUCH. T." She read it several times, frowning. It didn't look like Tom's handwriting, even printed. And it didn't sound like what he would say. They must have found him. Maybe somebody had come and seen him and called the cops. But what was the note for? How would anybody know about her? It sounded like a trap.

She rode her bike along the waterfront, trying to think. She stopped at a pay phone and called her mother. "Mom, it's me. Have you heard any more about Tom?"

"No. Not a word. And I'm so worried."

Shelley heard the tears in her voice, and felt a surge of sympathy. She must be feeling guilty as well as worried. If she hadn't refused to let Tom stay at home, this wouldn't have happened. She hung up, feeling guilty herself about not telling her mother what she knew. But it wasn't safe. Her mom was too impulsive. "Scatterbrained," her dad would say.

After a few minutes she called the police station. Pitching her voice as low as she could, she said, "Ipswich *Chronicle* here. Anything new on that kid who ran into Morton Barton? We know he broke out. Caught him yet?" She tried to sound tough.

"Nothing new, ma'am."

She thanked him, trying not to sound relieved. She hung up the phone and leaned against it in the hot booth, trying to think. Maybe he had gotten away. That note, though—that was not his handwriting. Maybe somebody was holding him to see if they could get a reward. . . .

Because she was near Genevieve's house, she decided to drop in. Not that it would help any, but Genevieve was always so calm and quiet, it made a person feel better. Genevieve did not know who she was. Shelley had showed up there one day with a phony story about Girl Scout cookies. Genevieve had ordered some casually, they had chatted a little, and she had shown Shelley her studio. Shelley had dropped in again from time to time. Genevieve never mentioned the cookies. After a while Shelley met Genevieve's father, Mort Barton, a bitter man in a wheelchair.

At first he had little to say to Shelley, but eventually he talked to her about the weather and things like that. Once he loosened up, he was quite nice.

Shelley didn't know why she had needed to meet Mort Barton. Somehow it had seemed important. And now that she knew Tom had not been driving the car that had crippled Mr. Barton, she kept trying to think of some way to clear things up.

She sat on her bike for a minute in front of the Barton house, staring at the ocean. Her dad would say mind your own business, don't stick your neck out. But her brother was her business. Maybe she ought to tell Genevieve the truth. Genevieve might have some ideas about what to do. That was risky though; she didn't really know her all that well.

She parked her bike and rang the doorbell. No one came, and she began to think no one was at home. Sometimes Genevieve put Mr. Barton's wheelchair in her van and took him for a ride. But as she was about to turn away, she heard the squeak of his wheelchair. He pulled open the door and stared up at her, not saying anything.

"I'm sorry, Mr. Barton. I thought maybe Genevieve was home. . . ." She wished she hadn't rung.

There was a pause, and then he said, "You might as well come in, Shelley. Genevieve's down at the gallery. If you don't mind sharing a Coke with me. . . ." He gave her his wry smile.

She took a deep breath. She had never been alone with him. What would they talk about? "Thanks, Mr. Barton, I'd love to." She opened the screen door and went in. Her knees were shaking. If he knew who she was! . . .

12

She followed Mr. Barton into the big living room, which overlooked the harbor. The radio was on, playing classical jazz. It reminded her of her father; he loved that kind of music.

Mr. Barton said, "Sit down, Shelley." He turned off the radio and maneuvered his chair over to a small bar set against the wall. When he opened the lower part of it, Shelley saw that it was a tiny refrigerator. He took out a bottle of Coke, and reached for a glass on top of the bar.

"I can do that," Shelley said, half getting up.

"No, no." He waved her back with a touch of impatience. "I may be crippled, but I can still open a bottle."

She flushed, realizing she had been tactless. If he hadn't been in a wheelchair, she wouldn't have offered to open the Coke herself.

He poured out the Coke carefully, brought it to her, and picked up his own half-finished glass of beer.

"Sorry," he said. "That was an oafish thing to say. I'm still touchy about what the doctor likes to call my immobile condition."

"You seem pretty mobile to me," Shelley said, but that didn't sound right either. She wished she hadn't come in. Hoping to change the subject she said, "I love the view from this room." She gestured toward the harbor. Out beyond the point several sailboats with bright-colored sails were heading seaward. The wind was good for sailing. She wished her dad hadn't sold their boat. Enid got seasick and was scared of the water as well, so he had said there was no point in keeping the boat.

He was looking at the sea, and his face looked sad. Shelley watched him out of the corner of her eye. He had a long face with a squared-off chin, and lines around the eyes and mouth; an emphatic face, she thought. How hard it must be for a man like that to be stuck in a wheelchair.

"I used to enjoy covering the races in my boat, when I worked for the paper." He said it matter-of-factly. "Some assignments were dogs, some were fun."

"I guess you miss it a lot," Shelley said. That probably wasn't the thing to say either, but she felt so sorry for him. If Tom could see Mr. Barton, he might not feel that having to spend a few months in that school was such a terrible thing. Only it was wrong for Tom to be locked up and not Buddy. She thought of something Tom had said yesterday: "Buddy trained me for that swimming meet at camp," he had said, "when I was a kid. He taught me to swim right. I won the relay." How could you think somebody was perfect just because he taught you to swim fast? She really didn't understand boys, not even Tom.

Mr. Barton sipped his beer. "Gen took some of her paintings over to the gallery," he said. "She's going to have an exhibition next week."

"That's great." She was glad they had moved onto safer ground. "I think she's a wonderful painter."

He smiled and glanced at one of the watercolors on the wall, a graceful sailboat, sails billowing, with an old motorboat beating along in its wake. "Everybody and his brother paints the coast, but I think Gen has something extra. She makes her own comment."

Shelley wasn't sure what he meant, but she liked having him talk to her as if she did understand him.

He leaned his head against the back of the chair. "What grade are you in this year, Shelley?"

"Eighth."

"Like it?"

Cautiously she said, "It's all right."

He smiled. He had a really nice smile that lit up his somber face. "I'll bet you like school, but it's not cool to say so."

She laughed. "Something like that, I guess."

He talked for a few minutes about the school he had gone to in Hamilton, where he had grown up. "We couldn't wait to get out, and now we go back for reunions and talk about how great it was." He shook his head. "The grass is always greener." He looked at her. "I don't think I know your last name, Shelley."

Shelley blinked. "Blaine," she said, after only a tiny hesitation. Blaine was her middle name. He wouldn't get any clues from that.

"Do I know your dad?"

"Oh, I don't think so. We haven't lived here too long. He works in Boston. In a bank." She felt her stomach tightening.

He looked at her a moment longer and then said, "I ask too many questions. Old newspaper habit."

She finished the Coke. "I have to go. Thank you very much for the Coke."

He saw her to the door, and she remembered just in time not to tell him he didn't have to. People did see people to the door when they left; it was normal behavior.

When she was safely outside, she got her bike and took off. That had been chancy. If he'd asked any more about her dad, she wouldn't have known what to say. She wished she had the nerve to ask *him* some questions, like whether he really thought he had seen two boys in the car that hit him. Or two people—he hadn't actually said boys. If he still thought he had, it would be easier to persuade people that Tom had not necessarily been the driver.

She rode back to the theater, but nothing had changed. She re-read the note. Tom wouldn't have said "all is well." But what was the point of a note if someone else had written it? She looked down at the beach and saw an old man getting out of an ancient-looking motorboat and wading ashore in rubber boots. At first she didn't think anything of it, but then she began to wonder if he could be the old man Tom had mentioned. She decided to follow him.

She was pretty good at tailing somebody. When she was in the fourth grade, she and her friend Jan used to shadow people they thought looked suspicious. They never got caught, and sometimes they found out very interesting things—like the fact that the new algebra teacher at the high school was seeing Miss McDougal, the first grade teacher. Shelley and Jan were the only ones who weren't surprised when Mr. Landers' divorce was announced in the paper, and a week later he and Miss McDougal were married.

She ducked behind some tall beach grass, as the old man trudged along the shoreline. She couldn't drop down to the beach without his seeing her, so she moved from cover to cover along the top of the cliff. Maybe he was the one who had turned Tom over to the cops. Her heart thudded with indignation. What a rotten thing, to act friendly and then betray somebody! Maybe Tom had told him about his sister, and he had printed that note trying to trap her, too. He looked more and more sinister to her as she crept along.

She was in the backyard of somebody's summer place that was boarded up now. The land here sloped down more gently to the water. The old man was walking toward what looked like a boat house. She remembered that this was the man to whom Genevieve had been giving painting lessons. What had Genevieve said about him, other than that he was talented? She'd better tell Genevieve that he was a snake. She lay on her stomach looking down at him. What had he done with Tom? Maybe he was holding him for ransom!

The man was right below her now, where the narrow, sandy path ended at the back of the boat house.

She inched forward a little more. She would have to get down there and look in a window or something, to see if he was holding Tom captive. The old man was whistling, and she thought, "I hope you choke."

Suddenly he tilted his head back and looked straight up at her. She tried to duck back, but it was too late. "'Lo there," he said. "You must be the sister."

"What?" she said, trying to sound blank. She was furious with herself for getting caught. Some detective she was!

"He's been worried about you. Come on down and say hello."

She had no choice. Maybe he would try to hold her too, but unless he had Tom tied up or something, the two of them ought to be able to handle an old man, even if he did look tough. She slid down the slope and faced him. "You can't get away with it," she said fiercely.

His blue eyes blinked. "How's that?"

"I know you've got him in there."

"'Course I've got him in there. Eatin' me out of house and home." He grinned. "Come on in. If he's left anything, you can have a bite with us. Does he always eat like that?"

She couldn't figure him out. Maybe he was just laughing at her. She followed him warily, ready to run if it became necessary.

He opened the door and stood back to let her in.

She wasn't going to be trapped that way. "You go first," she said.

"Shelley!" Tom stood there in the doorway beaming at her, as if she'd just come back from a vacation. "Where've you been? I was worried about you."

She exploded. "Where have *I* been! Where have *you* been? I was worried sick. I thought you'd been captured." She peered suspiciously at Harv. "Are you here on your own free will?"

"Of course I am. Harv's my friend."

"Well, you could have let me know!" She wanted to punch him in the stomach.

"We did. We left you a note."

"We, we, we! You didn't write that note."

Tom was beginning to look defensive. "What of it? Harv left it. . . ."

"How did I know? It wasn't your writing. I thought it was a trap."

"Well, you don't have to yell at me."

Harv took her gently by the arm. "Why'nt you come on in, Miss Shelley, and have a bite to eat. I should have thought about you spottin' that handwriting of mine. I'm sorry about that. You got any of that fudge left, Tom?"

"Yeah," Tom said. "Come on in, Shel."

"Well," she said. "All right." He would never know what she went through for him.

13

om couldn't understand why Shelley seemed mad. He had done his best to let her know he was okay. He couldn't send up a skywriter, for gosh sake. Girls could really be unreasonable, although he didn't expect it of Shel. It made him feel as if he'd done something wrong when he hadn't, and he hated that feeling. He'd been made to feel that way all summer.

But he didn't want to fight with her. He sat silent while Harv fixed her some lemonade, and got her some cookies and some fudge. Pretty soon her face began to relax.

"I was just so worried," she said, as if he had asked a question.

He started to answer and thought better of it. At school Tony always said, "Keep your mouth shut. That way you can't say anything that'll get you in trouble."

"Have another cookie, Miss Shelley," Harv said. "Mighty pretty day out there today. Lots of boats out."

Tom made an effort to sound like himself. "Shelley says she knows that lady you take painting lessons from, Harv."

They exchanged a quick glance before either of them spoke, and Tom thought *now* what have I said wrong? I can't do anything right.

But then Harv was saying, "Miss Genevieve's a fine lady."

"And a good painter," Shelley said. "At least I like what she paints. Not that I know a good one from a bad one. I like those watercolors. . . . Are they yours?" She was looking at the wall.

"Yep." He got up and pointed out two that hung on the seaside wall, two small similar watercolors of the cove. "Before and after. This one I did before Miss Gen showed me how to do it right."

The two of them were talking a blue streak about painting. It reminded him of the kind of chattery conversation his mother had with people she didn't know very well, talking to fill up the space silence made. He sat back and watched them. He'd gotten out of the habit of listening to polite talk. At the school you sometimes had serious conversation one on one; or maybe with a couple of guys. Otherwise it was just babble, usually a lot of people talking at once, and some who sat off by themselves and never opened their mouths. Not what you'd call conversation. Funny how quickly you could forget how people in the real world acted—like being polite for instance; Harv was polite. If you stopped to be polite at the school, you'd get stomped. Maybe he'd have to learn all over again to be civilized.

"Tom," Shelley said suddenly, "I almost forgot. . . ." She pulled a small piece of paper from her pocket. "I got Buddy's address in Maine. And phone number."

Tom jumped up. She almost *forgot?* The most important thing of all? "That's great! Now I can write to him and tell him what's up. Shel, will you wait while I do it, and mail it for me on your way home?" He grabbed the paper and looked at it. "Box 44 . . . What's that?"

Shelley looked over his shoulder. "Seven. Four four seven. She crosses her sevens, the way Europeans do." She grinned at Harv. "It's cool to do it that way. Box four four seven, Ellsworth, Maine, 04605."

"Harv, have you got an envelope and a piece of paper?"

Harv was already rummaging in a drawer.

"There's the phone number, too," Shelley said. "Ginna Fifield gave them to me. Maybe you ought to call, in case he's gone to New Haven already."

"Jeez! Ginna Fifield! You just asked her?" He'd seen Ginna Fifield last summer when she was an usher at the theater. He'd always wished he had the courage to speak to her.

"Sure. What's so great about Ginna Fifield?"

He shook his head. Shel had a lot to learn. "You might know she'd be one of Buddy's girls."

"Yeah," Shelley said. She was being sarcastic, but he didn't bother to wonder why.

He sat down at the table and wrote "Dear Buddy." Then he sat chewing the end of the ballpoint, trying to think what to say exactly. Maybe Buddy *was* at Yale. But he couldn't risk going out to a phone. He'd mark the envelope PLEASE FORWARD.

"I'll go over and take that note off the theater door," Harv said. "Before somebody wonders. You want to come along, Miss Shelley, so's our friend here can concentrate?"

"Sure."

He watched Shelley and Harv go. They acted like old buddies already. As if they knew things he didn't know. Oh, well. He bent over the paper. "I hope you're having a terrific summer." If he'd had another piece of paper, he would have crossed that out. He could imagine Buddy saying, "Summer's over, Sport," in that cool, amused voice. "Although I guess it's over, and you're ready for college. Buddy, I need real bad to talk to you, about what happened last spring. I'm in a real jam, which I guess you don't know about. But it can be straightened out if I can just talk to you." He paused, reading it over. It didn't sound right, but he didn't know how else to say it without coming right out. "Will you please call my sister Shelley and let her know when and where I can see you? It won't take much time, but I really have to see you. It's *urgent.*"

He read it again. "Good luck, and all that jazz. Yours sincerely, T." He didn't dare write his name. Somebody else might see the letter and guess who it was and call the cops. What if Buddy didn't know who T was, though? He might know a lot of people whose name began with T. He'd said "my sister Shelley," though. He'd know.

Tom was breathing hard. He was taking a chance. He could get Shelley into trouble, as well as himself, if Buddy wasn't careful. He added a postscript: "P.S. Please tear this up." He read it over twice, wishing he could come up with something better. He wished

Shelley had stayed with him while he wrote it; she was a good English student. Well, he wasn't trying to write a masterpiece, just something that would get through to Buddy. He was sure the whole problem was that Buddy just didn't realize what was going on.

He shot out of his chair as someone knocked on the door, looking around wildly for a place to hide. But already the door was opening.

A weatherbeaten face that looked vaguely familiar appeared in the doorway. "Harv? You home?"

"He . . . uh . . . went out," Tom said.

"Oh he did, did he." The man gave Tom a keen glance. "I guess you're the boy we fished out of the harbor."

Tom smiled weakly. "That's right. Thanks for hauling me out."

"Feelin' back to snuff, are ya?"

"I'm fine, thanks."

"Good enough. Well, I'll find Harv some other time." He waved with two fingers and left.

Tom sank into the chair, feeling weak in the knees. Was that guy really just looking for Harv or was he checking out Tom? Being on the run was hard on the nerves, all right. Everybody was a possible enemy. With shaky hands he put Buddy's letter in the envelope and sealed it. He printed the address and did not put down any return. He hoped Ginna Fifield knew what she was talking about. The phone number was on the paper, too. He wished he could call, but he didn't dare go uptown to a phone booth. Phone booths lit up like a spotlight, and you never could tell when a cop would cruise by.

He sat very still, half thinking, half listening for outside noises. He heard a sound. Somebody was coming. He tensed. Why didn't this stupid boat house have a back door! In the theater at least he had two ways to get out. Here he was trapped. Then he heard Shelley's voice and relaxed.

They came in, smiling and talking like old friends. Maybe they didn't realize how lucky they were to be able to walk around without worrying about who saw them.

"Here's the letter," he said.

"All right." She seemed to be over being mad at him. "I could send it certified, and then you'd know if he got it."

He thought about that. "I don't think so. It might make his parents curious. They'd want to know who it was from and all that."

Shelley picked up the piece of paper and studied it. "Tom, I could call this number and just see if Buddy's still there. Not say who I am or anything."

Why hadn't he thought of that? "Would you do that?"

"Sure. Why not?"

He fished out some change from his pocket. "How much do you think it would cost?"

"Oh, I've got some money." She thought for minute. "I shouldn't keep coming back here too often. How about, if I don't come back, you'll know he's still up there. And I'll mail the letter. If he's left, I'll come back and tell you."

"All right. Good." As she was leaving, he remembered to say, "Thanks, Shel."

She flashed a smile at him. "No sweat."

When she was gone, Harv said, "That's a girl with a good head on her shoulders, that is."

"Yeah," Tom said absently. He was trying to figure how long it would take her to call; how long before he could stop worrying about Buddy's being gone.

14

Shelley piled up quarters and dimes on the shelf in the phone booth. She hoped she had enough to call Ellsworth, Maine. She put in a quarter, dialed one and then dialed the number, saying the figures out loud to herself so she would get it right.

It didn't take so much money, after all. When she had deposited the right amount of change, she heard the phone ringing, and her stomach began to flip-flop. What if Buddy himself answered? She hadn't thought of a routine for that possibility. She could say one of his girlfriends had asked her to find out when he was coming home. . . .

"Hello?" It was a woman's voice, and she sounded so close that Shelley felt an impulse to duck. "Hello?"

"Hello." Shelley sounded hoarse.

"Yes? Who is it?"

"I was calling to find out if Buddy is there." She sounded idiotic, like a little kid. Now she'll ask who I am, Shelley thought, and I'll have to make up a name.

But the woman said, "Is this Patty?"

"Yes." Shelley crossed her fingers.

"He's already left for New Haven, Patty. Been gone a week. But he's coming home this afternoon to pick up his car. He had to leave it at the garage to get the fuel pump replaced. If you call him at the house, you might catch him."

"All right, I will." Shelley hoped she sounded like Patty, whoever she was. "Thank you."

"How's your mother, dear?"

"Oh, fine, thanks. Just fine."

"All over that summer flu?"

"Yes, all over it."

"I hope you didn't catch it. You sound a little hoarse."

Shelley cleared her throat. "Just a touch." Was this woman going to talk all day?

"We were sorry you didn't get up here before Bud left, but you call him at home, dear."

"Well, thank you very much. I'll do that. Goodbye." Shelley hung up and leaned against the phone. She was shaking. Whoever Patty was, she must have the inside track with Buddy's mother. So much for Ginna Fifield.

She moved out of the booth and gulped fresh air. Being a detective would be a very stressful occupation. She didn't think she was cut out for it.

Now what? She would have to go back and tell Tom. Then arrange for Tom to see Buddy. . . . She could spend hours trekking back and forth between Harv's boat house and the phone booth. There must be a better way. She had homework to do, after all; she couldn't hang around downtown forever.

She thought a minute and then went back into the booth and looked up Buddy's local number. He might just possibly be home already. She stood a moment thinking about what she would say. She did not believe, as Tom seemed to, that Buddy simply didn't know what had happened to Tom. Even if it hadn't been in the papers, people certainly talked about it. Tom and Buddy had gone to different high schools, Buddy here, Tom in Ipswich, but still, things like that got around.

She took a deep breath and dialed the number. She was about to hang up after the fourth ring, but suddenly a male voice said, "Yeah?"

"Buddy?" She made her voice as low as she could.

"Yeah? Who's this?"

"You don't know me, but I'm calling for a friend of yours who has to see you."

"What friend?" He sounded wary.

"Someone who has to talk to you. In your backyard, by the gardening shed, nine thirty tonight."

"Listen, I don't know what kind of a stupid act this is, but if you're calling for Jenny and she thinks she can trap me, tell her she's nuts. I'm not the only guy she's been with."

"It's not Jenny. It's someone you like. It will be to the advantage of both of you." The fingers on both her hands were crossed as she hung up.

Well, in a way you could say it would be to his advantage. He must be doing a lot of worrying that Tom would squeal. In fact, he must wonder why he hadn't already. Buddy was not the type to understand loyalty. If that's what you called it. She got on her bike and started back toward the beach. She didn't really understand Tom's loyalty or hero worship of Buddy. But Tom had always had heroes. When he was little, it was that astronaut that walked on the moon. Boys were weird.

She knocked a quick rat-a-tat-tat on Harv's door, and after a minute Tom cautiously opened it.

"Oh, it's you."

"Who else would it be?" She went in. Harv was cleaning paint brushes, and Tom had apparently been helping because his hands had streaks of blue and green. "Buddy's in town."

Tom sat down. He looked pale. "Then I've got to find some way to see him."

"It's all set up. Tonight at nine thirty in his backyard." She repeated the telephone conversation. "Some Romeo, Buddy is. Ginna Fifield, somebody named Patty, somebody named Jenny. . . ."

Tom looked a little sick. "What am I going to say to him?"

"Tell him you're tired of taking the rap for him. Tell him you're going to talk."

"What if he's too scared to say he was there? He's got a lot to lose—"

She looked at him. That was a sign of improvement, wasn't it? He was saying Buddy wasn't perfect after all. "Tell him you've got proof."

"I haven't, though."

"So it's your word against his."

"If I did, everybody would say how come I didn't tell them this before."

"Hold on a minute." Harv put his paint brushes in

the sink and came over to them, wiping his hands on a paper towel. The room smelled of linseed oil. "How about this: How about if I go with you and kinda lurk in the shadows, out of sight, and see what I can hear?"

Shelley reacted first. "A witness!"

"Maybe you can get him to kinda admit he was driving, just in conversation, you see? Everybody in this town, just about, knows me, and I don't think they'd expect me to tell a pack of lies."

Shelley was enthusiastic. "That's a terrific idea. You'd have no reason to lie. It'd hold up in court, wouldn't it?"

"Listen," Tom said. "Buddy's not going to deny it, not to me."

Shelley started to lose her temper, then gritted her teeth and made herself speak calmly. "What Harv means, Tom, is just if *he* can hear Buddy say he was there, he can swear to that if you need him to. So why don't you think up some questions that will get him to talk about it. Like. . . ." She paused to think. "You could say, 'Nobody's blaming you, Buddy. If I hadn't been so drunk, I'd probably have been driving myself.' Then he'll say, 'Yeah, but since it was me. . . .' See Tom? Something like that."

"Yeah, okay." To Harv he said, "I don't think there'll be any problem, once he understands. See, he's been up in Maine all summer. He probably hasn't any idea what's been going on. You could have just told him it was me that wants to see him, Shel. You didn't have to make up a story."

"Sure," Shelley said. She felt both exasperated with his insistence on Buddy's friendship, and very fond of him. He shouldn't have to be going through all this scary stuff, as if he were some kind of criminal. "I'll meet you guys at the corner of Ocean Street and Main at nine twenty-five. We can duck down the alley and come out by Buddy's backyard. Harv can loiter by the hedge. Me too." She gave Harv a warm smile. "Thanks a lot for helping us."

"My pleasure, Miss Shelley." He returned her smile. "I think we'll take the boat down to Proctor's landing. Nobody'll pay any attention to us that way. The Proctor place has been closed up since Labor Day. Then we just got a block and a half to where we meet you."

"Good thinking."

It'll be okay, she thought, as she rode her bike home. It's going to be hard on Tom, finding out what a creep Buddy really is. But he's got to grow up sometime. Maybe it'll all get settled soon now, and I'll get a chance to do my homework for a change.

15

Tom was nervous. He wanted to believe that Buddy was still his friend, and that things would turn out all right, but he really wasn't all that sure. When he let himself think about it, he knew it was unlikely that Buddy hadn't known what happened after the accident. But he couldn't bring himself to admit it out loud. His mother had never liked Buddy, never approved of Tom's having what she called "a sometime friend," older than he was, who, as she said, showed up when he felt like it and stayed away when he didn't. She had often disapproved of his friends. He missed her, though. He wished he could talk to her, tell her how sorry he was.

He had never told the guys at the school the real story about the accident. Not even Tony. He knew they would think he was some kind of patsy, taking the rap for his friend; and once they thought a thing like that about you, you didn't get any respect. It was important to be respected by the other guys at the school. Otherwise you'd be in real trouble.

He watched Harv patiently and carefully painting a tiny seagull in the watercolor of the cove. "I guess you think I'm stupid about Buddy, giving him the benefit of the doubt and all."

Harv didn't turn his head. He finished one tiny wing stroke and then said, "When you're friends with a fella, you go that extra mile, trustin' him." He picked up another brush and applied a small drop of orange to the gull's beak. "But I 'spose there comes a time when you got to face up to it. Some folks we think are friends, they aren't always just what we thought. We all disappoint each other from time to time."

Tom went to the window and watched the curling line of waves breaking on the sand like soapsuds. "My step-dad is a nice guy, but he's not real good with kids. He never knew what to do with me, so mostly he didn't do anything, except buy me stuff—new bikes, sleds, skis, stuff like that—and every summer they sent me off to camp. Buddy went to that camp, and he kind of took me under his wing, showed me the ropes. He let me do little things for him, and he kept the other kids from giving me a hard time. I was about the youngest boy there."

"That must have meant a lot to you," Harv said. "I can see that."

"I feel I owe him."

Harv glanced at him. "I expect you did. But it don't do to overpay your accounts." He stood back and studied his painting. "And I don't know if it does him any favor to let him get off scot-free. A person has to learn to take consequences. If he don't, sooner or later they catch up, and they're usually a whole lot worse."

Tom got a bottle of Coke from Harv's little refrigerator and went outside to sit on the steps. It looked like a long time from now till nine thirty.

16

Shelley went out the back door quietly. Her father and Enid were watching television. She had said she had to study, so it was unlikely they would notice she had gone out.

She felt jumpy. What if something went wrong, and Buddy or somebody called the cops? She didn't really think Buddy would risk that, but you never knew. It would be her fault if this thing turned out to be a disaster.

She looked at her watch. It was early yet. She rode her bike slowly past Buddy's house. All the lights were on, and the stereo was beating out a heavy metal sound. A girl threw open the front screen door and ran to the hammock on the porch, laughing the high, continuous, pot-user's giggle. A boy ran after her and threw her down on the hammock. She shrieked in delight, and the hammock rocked violently.

"Life in the fast lane," Shelley said to herself. "Yuk." She rode on down the street and came around to the narrow, tree-shaded street behind the house, and up the alley where she and Harv would wait for Tom. It was dark back there. All the better. A low hedge separated the property from the alley. If Tom waited back there by the shed, he'd be almost invisible. A back porch light lit up the steps to the house but not much beyond that. She nodded. The setup was perfect. All she could do now was pray. Maybe by this time next week Tom would be back home with their Mom, having his hot shower and his three square meals a day. Maybe he'd be happy again. But she knew he would never be quite the same kid he had been before the accident.

She looked at her watch and pedaled back to the corner of Ocean and Main. One minute to go. She watched the second hand. It was like being one of Tom's astronaut heroes, waiting through the countdown.

Once she thought she heard them coming, and she almost called out to them. Lucky she didn't; it was a man, walking fast, his jacket slung over his shoulder and held with one hand. Some corporation slave coming home late, she thought, a commuter like her dad. He gave her the quick glance people give each other in a small city, to see if she were someone he knew. She wasn't, but he said, "Hi," and kept going.

She looked at her watch. Five seconds.

Right on the dot, Harv and Tom came walking up the hill from the harbor. Tom was wearing a dark shirt, one of Harv's, she thought; it stretched tight across his chest. His face was set and tense. None of them spoke. She turned her bike and rode just ahead of them down the alley, then left her bike in the bushes on the far side of the alley.

Harv stationed himself in the shadows, his back against a telephone pole. Tom looked at both of them, nodded, jumped over the hedge and walked quickly to the shed at the back of the lot. Shelley couldn't see him. She lay on her stomach on the alley side of the hedge. If a car came along this way while they were here, they'd look pretty suspicious. But with any luck, it wouldn't be long.

A cool breeze off the ocean made her shiver. She turned her head for a moment to look at Harv. He had hunkered down against the telephone pole, so he wouldn't be seen from the yard. Her own heart was pounding, and she could imagine how poor Tom must be feeling. She shut her eyes tight. God, please make this go right. Tom is a good kid. Give him a break. She thought of Mary Alice Forbes last year in English class saying "The Lord helps those who help themselves," and Mrs. Adams saying, "That's not in the Bible, you know." It seemed like good advice, no matter who said it.

The back door of Buddy's house opened. She held her breath. He came out quietly, closing the door behind him and waiting for a moment at the top of the steps. He shaded his eyes with his hand, as if he were out in the sunlight. Then cautiously he came down the steps. He was wearing white shorts and a white shirt with short sleeves. Even in the dark he looked tanned.

He walked a little way into the yard, past the flower garden, then stopped and looked all around.

"Anybody here?" he said in a low voice.

Come on, Tom, come *on*, Shelley was saying in her mind.

Buddy half turned as if to go back into the house. A Marvin Gaye tape filled the yard with sound, then stopped abruptly. The front door slammed.

Suddenly, where there had been only shadows, Tom appeared.

"Buddy," he said in a low voice. "It's me."

"Who!" Buddy's voice was sharp and alarmed. "Who is it?"

"It's just me—Tom." Tom walked closer.

Buddy took a step backward. "What is this! I heard you were out, but I didn't think you'd. . . ." He broke off.

I heard you were out, Shelley thought. So much for Buddy's not knowing. Oh, poor Tom, poor Tom. . . . She ached to go out there and help him somehow.

"I never told them you were driving," Tom said. His voice was low but steady. Shelley felt proud of him.

Ask him one of those leading questions, she thought. Ask him, Tom. Make him admit it.

When Buddy said nothing, Tom went on. "But I have to tell them I wasn't. I mean I can't stand being locked up like that. So I thought we could work out some story. I don't want to get you in trouble, Buddy. You're my friend."

He blew it, Shelley thought. He should have stopped after "tell them I wasn't." Buddy would have said something. Now he'll stonewall it.

"I don't know what you're talking about." Buddy's voice was cold.

"Oh, come on, Buddy." Tom sounded suddenly very tired. "We're in this together. I mean it's my fault in a way; I gave you the keys."

"You were drunk as a skunk, Tommy." Buddy's voice was contemptuous now. "You never could handle yourself, Tommy. I always had to get you out of the messes you got into."

Shelley heard Tom's intake of breath. "You'll have to get yourself out of this one, Buddy." He turned away.

"It's my word against yours, Tom. Guess who's going to win that one." Buddy walked toward the back steps.

Tom didn't move for a moment, and then he followed him. "I protected you, Buddy."

Without looking back, Buddy said, "You always were a fool, Tom."

Tom grabbed Buddy's shirt and jerked him around to face him. "You bastard!"

Buddy knocked Tom's hand away. "You listen to me, Tommy boy, and you listen good. I'm on my way. I'm going to a good college, I'm going to law school, I'm going to make it. And don't you ever come around me again. You got it?"

"I've got it, Buddy." Tom's fist shot out.

Buddy staggered backward and fell onto the steps. Tom ran out of the yard, leaped over the hedge, and disappeared down the street.

Shelley heard Harv say, "Whew!" and then Harv too disappeared. She didn't move. She felt weak all over.

The back door opened, and a girl called, "Buddy?

Are you out there? Buddy?" She came out and saw him as he struggled up, holding a handkerchief to his face. "What's the matter? What you doing out here?"

"I fell down the steps." He jerked away from her as she tried to touch him. "Leave me alone."

"You're all bloody! Yuk!"

"It's just a nosebleed. Leave me alone." His voice sounded savage.

Shelley got to her knees and moved fast across the alley in a crouch. She grabbed her bike and fled down the alley.

17

Tom came down the beach road running, leaped over the Proctors' rail fence and cut across the lawn to their boat landing. Harv's boat bobbed gently at the dock. Without stopping Tom waded into the cold water up to his knees and leaned over, splashing water on his face and neck. His skinned knuckles smarted, but he hardly noticed.

He wrung the water out of the legs of his jeans and climbed into the boat. For a moment he thought how much he'd like to start the motor and just head out, anywhere away from here, just keep going till the gas ran out. And then? Yeah, and then. This was the place where the buck stopped, right here at this moment, in this boat. He couldn't play it by ear any more. He had to think.

Harv came so quietly, Tom didn't notice him until he was on the dock. Harv untied the boat and got in. Neither of them spoke. The motor coughed a couple of times and then caught, and Harv headed back to his own place.

As the boat settled into motion, Harv leaned forward and spoke above the noise of the motor. "You all right?"

"Fine."

Harv nodded. Nothing more was said until they were in the boat house. He locked the door and said, "Feel like some coffee?"

"Yeah, thanks."

Finally they faced each other across the small table, the coffee steaming and smelling good.

"I guess I blew it," Tom said.

Harv pursed his lips. "All depends on how you look at it."

"I didn't get him to admit anything, nothing you could use as a witness. I forgot all about it." He studied Harv's face. "I suppose Shel is furious, after she planned it all out for me and everything."

"I doubt she is," Harv said, "but I don't 'spose that's the point right now."

"The point being, what do I do." Tom took a long drink of coffee. "Buddy may have called the cops by now. He wouldn't get himself involved, but he could make an anonymous call. On the other hand, he might not. He might figure I'd really spill the beans if he did. Though he may think I'm still stupid enough not to get him into it." He shook his head. "I guess I've been some kind of stupid idiot. But I really thought, you know. . . ." He shook his head again. "He was a real good friend to me once. I guess he's changed. Or . . . I was thinking about it while I waited for you in the boat. Maybe it's just that he's figured out where he wants to go, like law school and all that, like his old man, make good money, be important, and he can't afford to let anything stop him." He looked up at Harv. "You know, for a minute there, I thought he seemed scared. In a way I felt sorry for him."

Harv looked over the top of his coffee cup. "Were you scared?"

"Right at first I was. Then I was mad and . . . sad. You know? Not just what he was doing to me, but what he was doing to himself." He finished his coffee. "Well, I have to get out of here. You could get into trouble harboring a fugitive. You've done an awful lot for me, but I have to move on."

"Where to?"

"I thought maybe I'd hitch a ride to Gloucester and see if I could get a job on a fishing boat. I don't suppose they ask too many questions. Or maybe, if I can't swing that, just get any old kind of job, dishwashing or garbageman or whatever, to keep going. It doesn't seem likely that I'm so important to law enforcement people that they're going to track me down in some other city, as long as I keep out of trouble."

"Not garbagemen," Harv said. "They're city employees."

"Oh. Well, there must be something, the kind of jobs people don't want." He pushed his chair back. "I ought to get started."

Harv shook his head. "Not tonight. If Buddy does call the cops, this is the night they'd be on the lookout."

"Oh. I hadn't thought of that." Tom frowned. "But I can't stay here. I could get you in trouble."

"Nobody's going to look for you here. If they do, I never asked who you are. You're just a stray kid that turned up on my beach and I gave you floor space for a couple days. I got one idea I'd like to make a stab at in the morning. If it don't work, then I'll run you down to Gloucester in the boat, speak to a couple guys I know with fishing boats. One of 'em owes me a favor. But you just lie low till then, okay?"

"Okay. But I don't know why you're doing all this for me. You don't even know me."

Harv grinned. "I don't have me a TV. I have to find my excitement where it shows up."

Later Tom lay stretched out on the floor in his sleeping bag, wide awake. He was surprised that he felt so calm. He would have thought he'd be all torn up, finding out that Buddy was willing to throw him to the wolves, but he didn't feel upset. He felt old and tired. He put his scraped knuckles to his mouth. They still stung. Hitting Buddy . . . he couldn't understand how he felt about hitting Buddy. Maybe it was that long summer at the school, all that pent-up feeling, coming out in one wallop. Hitting a guy didn't prove anything. Yet, if he had the scene to play all over again, he thought he'd still do it.

18

When Shelley let herself in the back door, her kitten jumped into her arms. The house was quiet except for the low drone of the television set. Enid was a late-night watcher. Shelley's dad usually went to bed by ten because he had to get up at five thirty to drive to Beverly and catch the commuter train to Boston.

Silently she went up the back stairs. The house was almost soundproof, solidly built by a sea captain in the late nineteenth century.

She had left the light on in her bedroom, so they wouldn't notice she was out unless they actually came into the room, which was not very likely. She got into her pajamas and sat down at her desk with her history book. But she couldn't settle her mind down. She kept seeing the faint outline of her brother standing there in the gloom of Buddy's backyard; she kept playing their conversation over in her mind, and then hearing the dull smack of Tom's fist hitting Buddy in the face.

She tried to look at the whole scene calmly and sanely. Tom had forgotten he was going to trap Buddy into an admission. He hadn't done that at all. He was in just as bad a fix as he had been before. And yet she had this feeling of triumph. Tom had changed, right there before her eyes in that backyard. Not just because he hit Buddy—that could have been just rage or whatever—but because he had been reasonable; he hadn't asked for anything that wasn't due him; and when he realized what Buddy was doing to him, he had said, "You bastard!" And he had taken responsibility for his part in the accident. He had grown up, kind of, right there in those five minutes. She ought to be worried about what would happen to him now, and she was worried, but she also felt good about her brother. The feeling she sometimes had, that in a way she was older than he was, was gone.

She flipped open her notebook and tried to concentrate on the Boston Massacre. But a couple of minutes later she was trying to think what Tom could do now. Shouldn't he go to the juvenile officer and tell him the whole story? He'd have to take a chance on being believed. It was better than being on the run and probably eventually getting caught anyway.

She jumped at the sound of a light knock on her door. It was her father, in his pajamas, with a glass of milk in one hand and a banana in the other.

"Hi," he said. "Can I come in?"

"Sure." She swiveled her chair around to face him. "Can't sleep?"

"No. Wide awake. Want a piece of banana?" He

broke off half of it and gave it to her, then sat on the edge of her bed. "I keep worrying about Tom."

"Oh. Well, it's no good worrying, I guess."

"The kid's only sixteen."

"Fifteen," Shelley said.

He sighed. "I don't know anything about him. I never did. I guess I'm a rotten father."

"Oh, Dad, come on." She was fond of him, but she really didn't feel up to boosting his self confidence, not tonight. "It's not your fault Tom got into trouble."

"When I married your mother, I hadn't thought at all about becoming an instant father. Tom wasn't much more than a baby, and he was cute, but I thought of him as your mother's problem, not mine."

Shelley ate a piece of banana and waited. Maybe I could get a job as a counselor, she thought wryly. Put a quarter in the slot and get a solution, guaranteed to work.

"You're a good kid, Shel," he said.

She made a face. "Thanks."

"I never had any trouble with you."

"Wait a while. I may grow into it."

He laughed and stood up. "I just wanted to say, I know Tom will never get in touch with me, but if you hear from him and there's anything I can do to help, anything at all, let me know. Will you?"

"Sure, Dad."

He kissed the top of her head and went out of the room.

Poor old Pop. She knew he meant it, but what was there he could do? There was only one person she could think of who might possibly be able to help.

And asking that person might be the very worst thing she could do. She closed her history book. Tomorrow was Saturday. With any luck she could get some studying in over the weekend, but tomorrow she would go to see Genevieve.

19

om had lost his feeling of calmness. He woke early, but Harv was already up, cooking eggs for their breakfast.

"Sleep well?" Harv said.

"Yeah." Tom felt a little embarrassed about having slept well. With all the momentous things he had on his mind, he should have tossed and turned all night. He got dressed quickly, and set the cups, paper plates, and forks on the little table. "I guess the sooner I get going, the better, don't you think?"

"Prob'ly. But there's somebody I want to talk to first. Won't take long."

"Is it about a job?"

"Could be. Might not."

Well, Harv talked that way. He wasn't trying to be mysterious. In his head Tom could hear Tony saying, "Don't trust nobody, pal. Nobody." But Harv had been a good friend so far, and it was hard not to trust people you liked. Of course, he'd trusted Buddy and been wrong. . . . All of a sudden, like a blow, the whole scene with Buddy came back to him. Losing a friend was like having somebody pull a chair out from under you.

"Eat hearty," Harv said. He always said that.

"I've gotten used to being here," Tom said. "It feels like I've been here a long time." Then because he didn't want Harv to think he was angling to stay, he added, "Time to move on."

"I've got used to having you," Harv said. "Enjoyed it." He finished his breakfast quickly, not lingering as he usually did over his second cup of coffee. "I've got this errand to do. You stay put. Lock the door after I go, and if anybody comes around, don't answer. Not that I expect anybody will."

Tom listened to the now familiar sound of the old boat coughing and sputtering and then settling into a steady roar. It sounded like a lot more boat than it really was. If I ever get out of this mess and make a little money, he thought, I'll get Harv a new motor for that boat; maybe even a new boat, with one of those fiberglass canopy things, so when he goes out fishing on cold and stormy days, he'll have some protection. An old guy like that ought not to be out there getting soaked through and chilled in all kinds of weather.

The sound of the boat faded away. It made him feel lonesome not to be able to hear it anymore. He tried to think what it would be like to work on a fishing boat. It wouldn't be any cinch, but he was strong and healthy; no reason why he couldn't do his share. He'd been fishing a few times with his father, and he'd gone out for lobster traps with the father of one of his friends, and he liked it.

He thought about that friend, Eric. They'd moved

away a couple of years ago and he'd never heard from him. He wondered what old Eric would say if he knew Tom had been locked up all summer. He thought about Eric's sister. She was a couple of years older than they were, and she'd never given him the time of day, but she sure was pretty. Tom had spent a lot of time fantasizing about her. He wished he could get over being shy with girls.

He got up and began to pace the room. Harv had only just gone, but it seemed like a long time. If Harv could line him up a job, that would solve a lot of problems. He wished Shelley would come by. He wanted to see her before he went away. She'd been real good about helping.

He rolled up his sleeping bag and packed his few things into the big paper bag he had brought with him. He'd leave the sleeping bag for Shelley to pick up.

He stood in front of Harv's small shaving mirror and tried to comb his hair differently. He combed it straight forward, so it came almost to his eyebrows. He looked like a punk rocker, with all that hair that should have been cut a couple of weeks ago. But as long as he looked unlike himself, that was fine. He wished he had some dark glasses.

He was leaning forward, studying his face, when a sharp knock on the door made him jump. He ducked down behind Harv's cot. It was a foldup affair and usually Harv folded it up and stashed it away against the back wall, but since Tom had been there, he had left it up so it could be used for sitting and talking.

Tom bumped his knee against the strong metal

frame. It seemed to him to make a noise you could hear for miles, but in fact it was only a small thud.

The knock came again, and a bass voice said, "Harv? You home, you good-for-nothin' son-of-a-gun?" In spite of the words the voice was amused. Whoever it was rattled the latch and knocked once more. Then there was a mutter, and silence.

Tom stayed on the floor—in case whoever it was decided to look in the window to make sure Harv wasn't there—or to check on whether a runaway boy was there. There was the fisherman who had hauled him off the buoy; that guy knew he was staying with Harv. By now a lot of people might know it; maybe even the cops.

He was uncomfortable. It was not a good bed for hiding under; too many braces and folding hinges. And he was too big. It reminded him of playing hide-and-seek when he was a little kid. Only this was real.

He moved to a hunched sitting position with his back to the wall, out of the line of vision of anyone looking in. What would happen if he gave himself up and told the whole story? If the cops and the juvenile people didn't believe him, if they said he was just trying to save himself, he'd be worse off than ever. And who was going to believe him after all this time? He banged his head sharply against the wall. What a jerk he'd been!

He got up cautiously, staying away from the windows. He wished Harv would come back. He felt as nervous and shaky as a bowl of Jell-O.

In the tiny kitchen he heated some water, and washed the dishes, carefully the way Harv did it.

If he got away, he'd have to be very careful with the few bucks he had left, till he could earn some money. He wished Shel would come. Maybe she'd lend him five dollars or so. She always saved her allowance. But it was the middle of the morning and she hadn't showed up. Probably she was disgusted with the way he'd handled the thing with Buddy. After she'd planned it out so well. He wished he had Shelley's good sense.

As he was hanging one of the cups on its hook, he froze. Somebody was unlocking the door. He whirled around, ready to fight or run or whatever he had to do. But there was a low whistle, and then there was Harv, coming in calmly as if nothing tense was happening.

"Whew!" Tom said. "You scared me."

Harv gave him a sharp glance. "Kind of nerved up, are you?"

"Somebody was here. I didn't go to the door."

"It was just Arnie O'Brien, wanted me to go bluefishing. I met him on my way back."

Tom waited. Then he said, "How did it go? Whatever you went for?"

In a guarded voice Harv said, "Good, I think. We got to stop off and see a fella for a minute. You packed up?"

"See what fella?"

"Fella I had a talk with. Ready to go?"

"Wait a minute, Harv. Aren't you going to tell me who this is?"

Harv shook his head. "Not right this minute."

Tom stared at him. "How do I know you aren't turning me in?"

106|

Harv met the stare. "Do you think I am?"

After a moment Tom looked away. "No. I don't. But I don't like to walk into something I don't know about."

"Trust me." Harv turned and walked toward the boat, and after a moment of hesitation Tom followed.

When they were in the boat, Harv said, "Don't blame you for being antsy about this, but this is the way it has to be. What I can tell you, if it don't work, you won't be any worse off. I'll take you straight to Gloucester and find that fella I told you about that thinks he owes me one. That suit you?"

"I guess it will have to," Tom said, but he felt very uneasy.

20

Shelley felt very nervous. She was sitting in a deck chair on the smooth stretch of grass just above the dock where the Bartons' boats were tied up. A white rowboat with green trim, and a motor launch with a fold-down ramp built into the stern, which could be bolted to a ramp on the dock just wide enough for a wheelchair.

"Harv built the ramps for us," Genevieve said. She filled Shelley's glass from the pitcher of lemonade on the small white iron table in front of her. "Now I can take Dad fishing, or just out for a ride. It means a lot to him."

"That's great." Shelley had arrived at the Barton's house just as Harv was leaving. She had been startled to see him there, even though she knew he took painting lessons from Genevieve. He had winked at her and said, "Hold on. Keep your cool, Miss Shelley," and then he was gone.

When she started to talk to Genevieve about Tom, as she had decided to do, Genevieve stopped her.

"I know about it," she said. "Harv told us."

"*Us?*"

"Don't worry, Shelley. It may work, and it may not. My father has been very bitter, and he has a lot to think over. But Tom won't be any worse off, in any case." She smiled at Shelley. "And I guessed some time ago who you were and why you came here." She reached out and patted Shelley's arm. "Relax. We're not monsters here."

Conversation after that had been hard. The thousand questions Shelley wanted to ask would not be answered, and she could not think of anything else. In her mind she tried to put together the possible plans they might have. None of them reassured her. "Should I leave?"

"No, please stay. And Shelley dear, don't worry so much."

But how could she not worry? She liked Genevieve and Mr. Barton, but after all she didn't really know them. And she didn't have to be psychic to know how Mr. Barton felt about the kid who had crippled him. She glanced behind her at the lower level of the house. Sliding glass doors, now partly open, led to the grassy area where she and Genevieve were sitting. A brick path bisected the smooth grass, and there were borders of chrysanthemums along the path. It was a pleasant place. She wished she could enjoy it.

"I took Dad to the doctor yesterday," Genevieve was saying. "They've scheduled more surgery for late October." Her attractive, tanned face looked concentrated, as if she were listening for something.

"Do they think they might be able to fix his back?"

"They don't know. Dad is skeptical, but I'm the optimist in the family."

"Oh," Shelley said softly, "that would be so great."

Genevieve gave her a quick smile. "Yes. It would."

The sound of a motorboat reached them. Genevieve tensed, and then seemed to make herself sit back and relax.

As the boat came around the bend, heading for the Bartons' dock, Shelley started to jump up. "That's Harv's boat!" She couldn't get out of the low-slung deck chair easily.

"Sit still, Shelley." Genevieve put out her hand, and her voice was low but insistent. "Sit still. Trust Harv."

"Trust him to what!" She could see Tom sitting in the stern of the boat, a little hunched over. "What are you doing?"

"Shelley. It's all right. Believe me. Harv is an honorable man, and he likes your brother. He believes him. Just sit tight and pray that it works."

Shelley felt cold. She was out of control of this situation and she hated that feeling. Not only out of control, she didn't even know what was going on.

As the boat came into the little cove Tom shaded his eyes, and saw her. He said something to Harv. Then he waved, not with enthusiasm but in a tentative way, as if he were puzzled.

Shelley waved back, but she wanted to jump up and warn him. Run, Tom! Get out of here! But she couldn't run on water. If this was a plot, it was pretty smart to bring him by water. Her heart was banging away in her chest as if she had just raced up a long hill.

110|

Well, if they planned to do anything bad to Tom, they'd have to do it over her dead body. She clenched her fists and waited.

"What's Shelley doing there?" Tom's voice was tight. The uneasiness he had felt on the short boat ride over here was building to panic. "What's going on?"

"Take it easy, boy."

Tom sat on the edge of the bow seat, trying to take in the scene as the boat chugged into the dock and Harv reversed the motor. Tom caught the dock piling and jumped out with the painter, as Harv cut the motor and stepped out. Shelley was coming toward them. Tom saw a woman he didn't know get up out of one of the chairs on the grass.

"Hi, Tom." Shelley looked nervous.

"What's going on?" he said. "Who's that?"

"That's my friend Genevieve, the artist. I told you about her."

"What are we here for?"

"For help," Shelley said.

"Will you tie 'er up, Tom?" Harv walked away, toward the woman, who was smiling at him.

Tom looped the line around the piling, still looking back at the scene on the grass. There was an odd sound in the house, sound he couldn't place. He stared at the open sliding doors. A man in a wheelchair maneuvered himself carefully over the short ramp onto the brick path. Then he looked up.

"No!" Tom said. "No!"

Shelley put out her hand. "It's all right, Tom. It's Mr. Barton and he wants to. . . ."

"You trapped me!" He gave Shelley a look that she

would remember the rest of her life. With one motion he unlooped the line and jumped into the boat.

"Tom!"

Harv came running. "Tom, it's. . . ." His words were lost in the sputter of the motor. It caught and died and then caught and kept on coughing for a moment, then steadied into its usual roar.

Shelley grabbed Harv's arm. "We've got to go after him. Quick, we can take Genevieve's boat. . . . Genevieve?" She turned to Genevieve, who stood beside her.

"No," Harv said. "We ain't going to chase him." He shaded his eyes with his hand and watched his boat growing smaller as it headed down the shore toward Gloucester. "No way are we going to chase him."

21

The traffic on the water was light. The tourist season was about over, and except for some Saturday sailors Tom had the coast to himself. The sky was overcast, and there was a light wind from the north.

He concentrated on the channel, trying to remember it from the times he'd gone sailing with his stepfather. That was a while back, though, because last summer he had been busy at the theater. The theater—maybe if he'd stayed there, instead of moving in with Harv, he wouldn't be in this fix. On the other hand, maybe he would. It might have been Shelley's idea, getting him to see that man.

He kept looking over his shoulder, expecting to see the big launch he'd noticed at that dock. Harv wouldn't let him just get away with his boat. The boat was how Harv kept going, fishing for food and a few bucks, getting around. He began to worry about Harv's boat.

He had no plan. If he went to Gloucester, he'd be easy to spot, with the boat. Maybe he ought to abandon the boat somewhere this side of Gloucester, and hitch, or walk from there. But if anybody alerted the police, and he was sure that man would, he was a goner.

He wiped salt spray from his face and realized he was sweating. That man in the wheelchair. He wasn't an old man. He was maybe the same age as his dad. Somebody had said he was a newspaper guy or had been. He was in that chair because Tom had gotten smashed and given Buddy the Audi keys. Seeing that man in that chair was a real shock; different from just hearing about it.

A few minutes later Tom throttled down and made a wide U-turn.

22

When he docked the boat, the only person in sight was the man in the wheelchair, sitting near the deck chairs and the little table on the grass. He had a bottle of Dos Equis and a tall glass in his hands. A pitcher of lemonade and another glass were on the table. As Tom walked toward him, he poured beer into his glass.

He looked up and nodded. "Have a chair. Want some lemonade?"

Tom sat down. His ears pounded, as if he had been diving. "I'm here," he said.

"Yes. Harv said you would be." The man studied Tom over the top of his beer glass as he sipped. "Harv told me your story. I'd like to hear it from you."

"It's not a story," Tom said. "It's the truth."

"Tell it."

Tom took a deep breath, clasped his hands tightly together to keep them from shaking, and began. Now and then the man stopped him with a question, but most of the time he sat quietly, listening, watching Tom's face, sipping his beer.

When Tom finished, he didn't speak for several minutes. Finally he said, "Do you do drugs?"

"No, sir."

"But you drink."

"Sometimes. I did."

"Get smashed pretty fast, do you?"

"Yes, sir."

"Probably better stay off the stuff then. It can be a pleasant diversion, or it can be dynamite."

"Yes, sir." But I didn't come here for a lecture on alcohol, he thought. Get to it.

The man let another long minute go by. "I'm not very happy about what's happened to me."

"Neither am I."

"It bothers you?"

Tom had been speaking in a low, controlled voice, but now his emotion burst through. "Of course it bothers me. What do you think? Especially now I've seen you."

"Yeah. Well, I'm not trying to rub your nose in it. Or maybe I am, a little. I've had some pretty savage feelings."

Tom turned his head away. He couldn't stand to look at the man's eyes. He wanted to run and run and run.

"It seems to me you share quite a lot of responsibility for the accident, even if you weren't driving."

"I know that."

"On the other hand, you've been locked up, and your friend got off scot-free. That isn't very fair. I admire you for not squealing on your friend, but on the other hand I think it was stupid. That kind of King Arthur stuff, I don't think it goes down in the real world. Maybe I'm a cynic—newspapermen are supposed to be. But I don't think you did your pal any good, letting him get away with a crime. Do you?"

"I guess not. I didn't see it that way before."

"But you do now?"

"Well, the way he acted. . . ."

"Did you expect him to be grateful?"

"Of course not."

"Maybe you did, without realizing it. Maybe you wanted to prove what a terrific friend you were, make him indebted to you. We all play those games with ourselves."

The conversation was not going the way Tom had expected it to. He wished the man would say whether he was going to call the cops or what.

"It was stupid to take the blame. It was stupid to run away," the man said.

"So I was stupid."

The man smiled a tight little smile. "And you wish I'd lay off the psychology and get to the point. Harry Felton is your juvenile officer, isn't he?" When Tom nodded, he went on. "I can call him, and you can tell him what you've told me. Or you can leave here and fend for yourself, a fugitive."

Tom frowned. "You mean I decide?"

"You decide."

Tom stared out over the water. The hearing was coming up next week, Shelley had said. He had run away. He could picture that judge, scowling at him and saying, "You have been irresponsible from start to finish." Even if they could get Buddy to admit he'd been driving—and Tom doubted if they could; Buddy's father would get him a hot shot lawyer—even then they'd probably send him back to the school. Maybe put him in max.

But if he kept on running, what kind of life would he have? When he thought about it, he felt old and tired.

He looked at the man in the wheelchair. "You can't run away, even if you want to, can you."

There was a glimmer of something in the man's eyes that Tom couldn't read. "Plenty of times I've wished I could."

Tom took a deep breath and closed his eyes for a moment. "I guess you can call Mr. Felton."

Mr. Barton put his beer glass on the table. It made a clinky sound. He poured lemonade into a clean glass and handed it to Tom. "I'm glad you said that."

Tom held the cool glass in his hand. Out on the water a sailboat with a striped sail was tacking into the breeze. "They'll probably lock me up again."

"I'll testify for you."

Tom's head snapped around; he stared at Mr. Barton. "*For* me?"

"I believe you. I'll say so in court."

"Wow," Tom said softly. "I never expected *that*."

"Neither did I, to tell you the truth. But I think it's time your friend Buddy answered some questions."

"He'll deny it, and they'll believe him."

"I doubt that. I've already told the police I was pretty sure there were two people in that car."

"He'll say I was driving."

"What Harv heard the other night sounds fairly damaging to Buddy. He'll tell it in court."

Tom felt a slow, rising excitement in his chest, but he was almost afraid to let it go. He shouldn't get his hopes up. "If they *did* let me off," he said, almost unwilling to say the words out loud, "if they put me on parole or something, maybe my mom would let me come home. . . ."

"Shelley is sure she would."

"She gets pretty teed off at me sometimes, but maybe I could make it up to her." He looked at Mr. Barton. "I can't ever make it up to you though."

Mr. Barton shrugged. Then suddenly he grinned. "Don't worry, I'll exploit your guilt. I can already think of a dozen ways I can put you to good use. Can you sail a boat?"

"A catboat. My step-dad had a catboat. I've never tried anything bigger."

"Well, you can learn. I've got my sailboat in dry dock, because I couldn't stand to look at it, now I can't sail her myself. But if I had a hand, that'd be different. Gen isn't keen on sailing, too much work, she says."

"Listen," Tom said, "I'll sail you anywhere you want to go. As soon as I'm sixteen, I'll drive you wherever you want to go. I'll do anything you want."

The man laughed. "Don't make too many promises."

"I mean it," Tom said. "Honest, I mean it."

"Why don't you go up to the house now and get those people to join us. Your sister has been going crazy with suspense. She didn't want us to set you up like this, by the way; it was Harv's idea. He had to talk me into it. Shelley was scared to death about it."

Tom stood up. "I guess I've made a lot of people worry a lot."

Mr. Barton just looked at him without answering.

Tom started toward the house, but before he had gone far, Shelley burst out and came running toward him.

"Tom!" She was almost in tears.

He grabbed her and hugged her tight. "Take it easy, Halfie. I think it's going to be okay."

BARBARA CORCORAN was born in Hamilton, Massachusetts, and graduated from Wellesley College. Her first job was stuffing envelopes at the University of North Carolina Press for twenty-five cents an hour, a profession she did not pursue for any length of time. Subsequent occupations over the years have included playwright, electronics inspector for the Navy, cryptanalytic aide for the Army Signal Corps during World War II, manager of a celebrity service in Hollywood, and teacher.

Ms. Corcoran has written more than fifty books for young readers, including the Camelot title, *You Put Up with Me, I'll Put Up with You*. She presently lives in Missoula, Montana.